DREAM VOYAGER

Books by Thomas Locke

THOMAS LOCKE MYSTERY Series
The Delta Factor
The Omega Network

SPECTRUM CHRONICLES Series
Light Weaver
Dream Voyager

THE SPECTRUM CHRONICLES
2

DREAM VOYAGER

THOMAS LOCKE

BETHANY HOUSE PUBLISHERS
MINNEAPOLIS, MINNESOTA 55438

Cover illustration by Joe Nordstrom

Published by Bethany House Publishers
A Ministry of Bethany Fellowship, Inc.
11300 Hampshire Avenue South
Minneapolis, Minnesota 55438

Printed in the United States of America.

Library of Congress Cataloging-in-Publication Data

Locke, Thomas.
    Dream voyager / Thomas Locke.
        p.   cm. — (The spectrum chronicles ; #2)
    Summary: After tangling with pirates in space, Consuela awakes in a hospital on the world Avanti, where her beloved Scout friend Wander stands accused of being a renegrade.

    [1. Science Fiction.] I. Title. II. Series: Locke, Thomas.
Spectrum chronicles ; 2.
PZ7.L7945Dr   1995
[Fic]—dc20   94–38986
ISBN 1–55661–433–0   CIP
                                                             AC

This book is dedicated to

Jacques and Odile Dupin

through whose open-hearted welcome
I have come to know and love
their land.

THOMAS LOCKE is a delightful addition to Bethany's team of writers, and his exceptional creativity has taken flight in this latest book for teens. An avid fantasy and science-fiction reader himself, Thomas Locke offers the young adult audience a thrill-packed tale with a spiritual message that spans both worlds.

– One –

Consuela was delighted when Rick could not come to pick her up, and it had nothing whatsoever to do with his reputation. She was happy because it meant he would not be able to see where she lived, or how she lived, or with whom. Consuela did everything she could to separate her school-life from her home-life.

Not even the girls on the cheerleading squad had ever visited her home. This was very odd, because the girls took turns inviting the squad over for Wednesday night meals. When it was Consuela's turn, she treated the group to dinner at the local hangout, saying her mother was down with the flu—though the extravagance cost her a month's wages. Which was another odd thing about Consuela—some afternoons and Saturdays she worked for the most expensive women's boutique in town. One of the girls discovered it only because her parents took her there for a sixteenth birthday ball gown, and who should wait on them but Consuela. When the other girls asked her about it, Consuela played it very casual and grown-up, saying it was easy work, she met a lot of interesting people, and it gave her money to buy clothes. Which was a strange thing for her to say, since Consuela had only a few outfits that any of them had ever seen, but she mixed and matched them so cleverly that it was really hard to tell. And none of the clothes looked expensive enough to have been bought where she worked.

Had she been less attractive or friendly, it would have been easy to make her an outsider. Not that she was beautiful—not at all. Consuela's features were too strong for her face to be really beautiful. Her black hair hung long and full and simple, without any of the curls or flounces or shingled, frosted layers that were popular with the other girls. She wore no jewelry and little makeup. But there was a mystique to Consuela, a sense of strength and depth that drew people to her.

"I feel like I can tell her anything," her best friend Sally told the others one lunchtime. "I mean, *anything*. I don't know why, but I bet if I told her I was hooked on drugs or moving to Morocco, she wouldn't bat an eye."

"She's seventeen going on ninety-seven," somebody else agreed.

"She is the most unshakable person I've ever met," Sally went on, trying to put into words what she really couldn't understand herself. "She just listens to whatever I want to tell her, like she's taking it all really deep inside. I never get the feeling she's out to put me down."

"I know what it is," another of the girls declared. "She has this mysterious past. She's been all around the world, seen it all, done everything, and she's just too modest to talk about it."

"I like her," someone declared, and then realized what she had just said and covered it with a laugh.

Had Consuela heard what they said about her, she would not have believed it. Her own feelings about herself were very different. To Consuela's mind, her life at school was one big lie.

But she didn't want to think about those things now. Not when she was rushing from the bus stop to the carnival entrance, where she was to meet Rick Reynolds, captain of the football team and the best-looking guy at school. Consuela turned the corner; up ahead the road was lit by the garish carnival lighting. Under the flickering sign stood Rick, and she felt a little thrill of excitement at the thought that he was waiting there for her. For *her*.

Now was certainly not a time to be worrying about all the stuff she kept hidden from the world. Consuela put on her very best smile and hoped he would look happy to see her. Then he turned and spotted her, and his own face lit up with a satisfied smile. Yes, things were certainly looking up.

Wander climbed down the bank as carefully as he could. He was still unused to wearing the scout's robe of pale blue and wished he could return to his everyday clothing. But scouts were required to wear their robes at all times, on and off duty. So Wander gathered up the folds, tucked them into his belt, and tried hard not to slip on the icy embankment.

The tree trunk brought back a flood of memories. So many hours he had sat there, looking across the floodlit expanse at the great vessels resting in their gravity nets, eager to be released to fly up, up, up and away. Since his childhood, Wander had known only one dream, to fly with them.

He checked his chronolog, a habit that was useful because it masked his burgeoning abilities from those who did not share his sensitivity. But here in the splendid isolation of a frozen forest, he had no need to check the time.

He could hear the pilot's droning count as clearly as if he were still in the instruction hall, his headpiece plugged into the amplification system.

The pilot gave the captain the formal two-minute warning. Wander brushed snow from the trunk and seated himself just as the first glimmer of power emanated from the ship's circular base. Four other ships awaited their place on the thruster shield, all freighters bound for the Outer Rim. Passenger vessels used daytime departure slots while the port was fully active. At night things slowed down, and the port's two shields were given over to freight and private vessels unwilling to pay for daytime slots.

A thrilling hum lifted the hairs on the nape of Wander's neck as the ship's thrusters built up power. The charged smell of ionized air lifted over the energy fence and sent Wander spinning back to earlier times, but not for long. At the one-minute count, the power-up reached quarter thrust, and the first faint shimmers of the gravity net came into view. This was the part Wander loved best. The air became so charged that faint blue tendrils of disconnected power drifted behind each movement of his hand, while around him the frozen tree limbs glowed like living sapphires.

Thirty seconds, half thrust. The energy net was shining all about the ship, like interconnected weavings of light. The strain of holding the ship earthbound caused the net to shine with brilliant silver fire. Fifteen seconds, three-quarters thrust. The fire-net was now so fierce that Wander had to squint to hold it in focus. His robe had become charged to the point that it billowed slightly from his body. The entire landscape about him was shining with an eerie luminosity. The humming was so intense that his chest vibrated. The final countdown began.

Seconds flowed more slowly through his mind. He remained connected to the pilot as the ship's power was extended outward, outward, outward, and the heavens split open, a great whirling seam just above the ship, revealing the nothingness into which the ship would leap. Two seconds remaining now and the pilot's voice was as slow as the thrumming ship's chronographer, one second and the final destination was brought into tight focus. Time slowed to an almost frozen moment as the energy net was released and the ship began the stretching, reaching, flowing motion that extended it upward and into the seamed opening, through the void and to its destination.

Then it was over. One moment there, the next gone. To the world the time required was less than a second. To Wander it was a moment beyond time, his body registering earthbound time, his mind connected to the pilot and his search through the known universe for the destination, until the moment came for the stretching, reaching climb. Then his mind snapped back to earthbound focus, and he breathed for what felt like the first time in days.

It was an experience he never grew tired of.

Wander rose to his feet, brushed the snow from his robes, and struggled back up the slope. His control-tower watch began in less than an hour, and he had to make his way around the energy fence.

Still, there was a great vantage point by the water reservoir. If he hurried, he could stop and see one more freighter depart.

"Hey, Consuela, great, you made it!" Rick's smile was legendary, as were his looks and his accomplishments.

And his reputation.

Consuela found her resistance melting under the power of his smile and eyes. Earlier that week, after Rick had sauntered up to where Consuela sat studying in the school library and asked her out, Sally had described his reputation in detail. Rick had the habit of coming on strong, charming a girl, taking what he wanted, then dumping her. The story was, Sally told her, that Rick had fallen head over heels for a girl the year before. She had dropped him hard. Since then, Rick had played it cool and tough with every girl in reach.

"Hello, Rick," Consuela said, stepping up in front of him. "I hope I haven't kept you waiting."

"No problem. Come on, what do you want to try first?"

She laughed as his arm slipped possessively around her waist and drew her close. Despite herself, all the warnings were swiftly slipping away in the excitement of the moment. She could hardly believe it was happening to her. A date with Rick. Maybe it would be different with her. Maybe he would decide that they made a great couple. Maybe . . .

If only she could keep him from finding out the truth.

Rick took her laughter as a signal to draw her closer still. "You like roller coasters?"

"Sure." She had never been on a roller coaster in her life. She had hardly been anywhere or done anything. The depth that other girls noticed in her did not come from incredible experience—at least, not the kind of experience they imagined. Her strength came from simply having to cope.

Her mother was an alcoholic. Her father had left home so soon after she was born that Consuela had no memory of him at all. The social worker responsible for her case had come within a hair's breadth of taking her away and sticking her into foster care a dozen times or more. Consuela had survived because Consuela was a survivor. But inside, where only she could see, Consuela felt ashamed about her home-life and terrified that someday somebody would discover who she really was.

Consuela had only two friends who knew the truth. But Daniel and Bliss had moved to Chicago when she was thirteen, and although they called her every week and wrote almost as often, all the experiences they had shared had faded. Sometimes she would remember things and feel as though they had been nothing but the fantasies of a young girl. And like the dolls that Consuela never had, she felt the memories needed to be put away now that she was growing up.

When Daniel and Bliss returned for a visit, which happened once a year, things became clearer, but only a little. Daniel always tied the memories into his talks about faith, and all that didn't seem to have much place in Consuela's world.

As she grew older, Consuela found it easier not to think much about those things at all. With the years, the memories and the faith and the talks faded until they were no more vivid than the recollections of a movie seen years before.

Rick shouted a hello to some friends and stopped to trade insults. Consuela was content to stand and watch and listen, her habitual small smile hiding everything inside. To others, she appeared incredibly mature. To herself, she seemed the loneliest person on earth.

Rick refused their pleas to join the others and pulled away, but not before one of the other girls gave Consuela a knowing smirk. In that instant the thin veneer of calm that shielded her shattered. For a brief moment Consuela faltered, the joy vanished, and she was simply a scared young girl walking through the tawdry garishness of a cheap carnival.

"Hey, listen, if you want to go with them, it's fine with

me," Rick said, misunderstanding her grave expression. "I just thought, you know, it'd be more fun to be alone."

"It's fine," she said, struggling hard to recapture the moment. "I'm glad you asked me out."

"Likewise." Rick Reynolds, senior class president, captain of the football team, and student most likely to succeed at whatever he decided to do with his life, smiled down at her. "I mean, when I saw you trying out for the cheerleading squad last month, I thought this was one babe I had to get to know."

Babe. It was the first time anybody had ever called her a babe. She wasn't sure she liked it, even from Rick. But before she could say anything, he stopped at the end of the line waiting turns on the roller coaster and said, "Wait right here. I'll go get us tickets."

She watched as another group stopped to talk with him. He turned and pointed back in her direction. She gave them the smile and wave they expected, although she knew none of them. But everybody knew Rick and wanted to be seen with him. Rick's dad ran some big company. He drove an almost-new Corvette. He dressed like some ad in the magazines Consuela saw around the shop—Armani jeans, Doc Marten's shoes, silk-and-cotton knit shirt, a bomber jacket slung casually across one shoulder. Last week his picture had been in the city paper with an article about his acceptance of a full football scholarship to the best university in the state. No question about it, Rick was a guy on his way to the top.

He came trotting back, all eagerness and charm. "Hey, I'm really sorry about not being able to pick you up. But like I said, the coach always keeps us late on Fridays."

"It was no problem, really," Consuela replied. "I got a ride." Right. With her friendly bus.

"Good. Where is it that you live, anyway?"

"Westgate," she replied, naming the nice development that bordered the tenement area where she lived. It was only by dint of a shadowy school borderline and her own excellent grades that Consuela was permitted to go to the Nathan Henry High School at all.

"Nice," he said approvingly. "I live in Northside."

"I know," she said quietly. Sally again. Her friend was a font of useful information.

For reasons Consuela could not understand, Sally had adopted her the first day of school. Sally was everything Consuela was not—vivacious, eager, happy, lighthearted. Her father was a doctor, her mother a dedicated nurse.

Sally had insisted that they try out for the cheerleading squad together. Consuela had agreed with her plan that either they would both be accepted or neither would join, seeing it as the perfect out; she knew there was no chance that she would be accepted. When they both were selected, she found herself unable to back out, and then to her surprise found that she really enjoyed it. Yes, it was silly. But all kinds of people suddenly said hello to her in the halls, and she was accepted into a group of girls that she would never have dared speak with before.

And now a date with Rick. It was all happening so fast.

Rick was finding the night to be very rough going.

He was not used to having to work so hard. He was not used to having to force anything. Girls normally gushed over him. All he had to do was go with the flow. But not Consuela.

Whatever else this girl was, she was no conversationalist. As a matter of fact, Rick was not really sure why he had asked her out in the first place. Maybe it was the mystery that hung in the air around her like a veil. Yeah, that was probably it. Consuela had something about her that made her stand out from the other girls at school.

When they finally reached the head of the line, Rick let her slide into the roller coaster's padded seat first so he could watch her reaction. Most girls showed some kind of nerves. But not Consuela. She looked about and showed nothing more than a sort of mild curiosity. Rick slid into the seat beside her and wondered if maybe the whole date was a total loss.

The car started off to a chorus of screams. Consuela's eyes widened slightly as they began to climb. The wind caught her long dark hair and tossed it so that it was flung into his face. She pulled it back. "Sorry."

"No problem. Have you been on this one before?"

She hesitated, then replied, "I've never been on a roller coaster in my life."

"You're kidding."

"Why would I kid you about something like that?" She seemed oblivious to the shouts and squeals rising before and behind them as the climb continued up above the entire carnival.

"I mean, aren't you a little scared?"

"Of what?" She seemed truly baffled by his question.

But before he could reply, they crested the ridge and plunged down. Rick cast a quick glance her way and was somehow extremely pleased to see her smile. For reasons he could not explain, it really mattered to him that he break through that impenetrable shell of hers. Then he turned back and gave in to the thrill of a three-second free fall.

A swoop at the bottom, an impossibly sharp curve, an upside-down loop, and then into the tunnel. Blackness surrounded them, and the air was filled with the sound of semi-fake fear. Then came the rush out of the tunnel, screaming around the final bend, and braking to a halt.

"Want to go again?" Rick asked, only half joking, his eyes still adjusting to the flashing lights. He turned to the seat beside him and felt his entire body go cold.

Consuela was no longer there.

–Two–

Wander sat on what he thought of as his own little mound and readied for the next two-minute countdown. No one else ever came out here, especially at night, so he was safe in laying claim to this spot. Certainly no one from the port came this way. All the roads led back in the other direction, toward the city. The unfortunates who lived in the hovels beyond the woods considered the area to be haunted.

Before him the water reservoir lay frozen solid and frosted with snow. Wander liked watching the seasons reflect the power of a launch. In summer the lake reflected launches in mirror stillness, as though a second ship were fired toward the center of the earth. In winter the ice sparkled blue and alien with discharged kinetic energy.

Wander had been coming here since he had learned to walk, drawn by the voices and the power that he then thought everyone could hear. Now he knew better and was learning to live with the loneliness that his special abilities created.

Suddenly he sensed that he was no longer alone.

He whirled and found himself facing a girl. A *beautiful*

girl. Dark hair, sharply defined features, tall and poised, with dark wide-open eyes. Eyes that spoke of total incomprehension.

And she wore a scout's robes.

She looked at him with a gaze that only half saw, and asked, "Where am I?"

He had to laugh. For a scout to ask that question was just too funny. Then he remembered something from the morning's class. "You're the newcomer, aren't you?"

"What?" She gave another start as she looked down at herself, lifted one fold of palest blue, and asked, "Am I dreaming?"

"The mind-lag must have hit you really hard," Wander said sympathetically. "I hear it can be rough the first few times." He hesitated, then made the embarrassed confession, "I've never been off-world before, so I wouldn't know."

The girl made a genuine effort to draw him into focus. "Who are you?"

"Wander. I'm in your scout class," he said patiently. "That is, if you're the newcomer. Where are you from?"

"Baltimore," she replied, looking down at her robes again.

"Never heard of it," he said, "but there are so many worlds, I guess that's no surprise."

"So many what?" Then the ship's pilot droned the formal two-minute warning, and the girl gave a little gasp and jumped a good foot off the snow. "What was *that*?"

Wander stared at her. "You heard it?"

She was still searching the surrounding fields. "Heard *what*?"

"They said the newcomer was supposed to be really something. I guess you'd have to be, if they let you skip the first cull." He slid over, trembling in the excitement of suddenly not being the only one. The odd boy out. The lonely kid who heard what others refused to believe truly existed. "Come sit down. The show's starting."

In dazed confusion, the girl walked over and sat beside him. Then the first hazy impressions of the gravity net appeared about the ship, and she cried aloud.

Ninety seconds, came the pilot's drone, and again she gasped, and Wander felt a chill go through his entire frame. She had indeed heard it.

The icy landscape spreading out before them began to pick up the energy discharge caused by the ship's thrusters straining against the shield's gravity net. Wander risked a glance her way, saw eyes impossibly wide and a slightly opened mouth, and suddenly realized she had never seen a launch before.

He raised his hand and said quietly, "Look at this." With a gentle loose-limbed motion, he extended his arm and flung his hand outward. A cloud of bluish energy wafted out and over the lake. He turned back and was rewarded with a look of utter disbelief. But no fear. Wander was sure of it without really understanding why. Although the scene was utterly new, the girl showed no fear.

He turned back, unable to stop grinning, and waited for the launch to continue. For some reason, having her here beside him made it feel as though he were seeing it all for the very first time.

She gasped when the first tendrils of snow lifted from the field and began their ghostly dance. As the energy friction grew in power, breaths of azure light passed from one dancing cloud to the next, and the entire frozen vista glowed as though lit from beneath.

Then the fifteen-second interval was marked, and time began to stretch, and the girl reached over and took his hand. Wander could scarcely believe it was happening, nor understand what it meant, that here beside him sat another person who required neither headset nor amplifier to tie into the moment of transition. The moment stretched out, granting him the thrill that he had known a hundred thousand times and never tired of, feeling his body count the normal seconds while his mind was let loose to know an endless instant's freedom.

Almost.

Perhaps it was because of the training he had begun. Perhaps it was the heightened sensitivity he felt, having this girl seated beside him holding his hand. Whatever the reason, Wander found himself able to search out the niggling impression that he had always known but not identified. The moment of blissfully being freed from time's chains was not complete. The bonds were stretched, but not broken. Yet his heart yearned for something more, and in that stretched instant of heightened awareness, Wander knew that a true freedom was possible. He *knew* it.

Then the swirling lightning-flecked clouds opened to reveal the maw of nothingness, and in his heightened time-sense Wander watched the gravity-net dissolve, permitting the ship's thruster power to rise from the shield, a brilliant ball of pulsating force, transforming the ship into a lance of molten gold that stretched higher and higher and higher into the maw, through the infinite nothingness, to touch the shield at its final destination, for a moment shorter than the smallest measurement of earthly time resting on both planets simultaneously. Then the ship departed, the maw closed, the energy dissipated, the snow flurries settled, time returned to its normal boundaries, and the night drew in about them.

It was a very long moment before the girl took a ragged breath and sighed, "Wow."

The feeling was so glorious Wander felt free to say anything he wanted. His own shackles of shyness were momentarily gone. "That was your first launch, wasn't it?"

"Yes." Her response was a breath, a cloud of sweet air wafted out so softly he could barely hear it.

"I'm glad I could share it with you." He looked down to his hand, which still held hers, wishing it could stay there forever, knowing she would come alert in a moment and take it back.

She looked about, then asked to the night, "Napoleon? Cousteau? Daniel?" She hesitated a moment longer, then called, "Rick?"

"We're alone," Wander replied. "Nobody comes here. If any of the other scouts heard we did this, they'd scorn us."

"The other what?" Still she searched around her. "Have you seen a rabbit around here?"

"There are no animals here," he replied questioningly. "There haven't been since the port became operational." He examined her face. "The mind-lag really has affected you, hasn't it?"

"I guess so," she sighed, then shivered. "It's cold."

"Is it not winter where you came from?"

She shook her head. "Autumn."

"Here spring is less than two months away. This is the time of the hardest frost. What is your name?"

"Consuela."

When she shivered again, he stood and said, "We'd better go back. I'll have just enough time to help you find your quarters before I go on watch."

Consuela rose unsteadily to her feet, but did not release his hand. "Where did you say we were?"

He gave her slender fingers a gentle squeeze and said quietly, "Come on, try and walk a little faster. Everything is going to be all right."

–Three–

"Gone? Whaddaya mean, gone?" The carnival manager was a fleshy jowled, cigar-chomping little man in his late fifties. His office smelled of ashes and burnt coffee and old sweat. "Nobody can get outta those seats when the ride's going. You saw that padded bar. We had it specially made. It goes down automatic, stays down 'til the ride stops. You can't stand up, much less get out." He leaned heavy forearms on the paper-strewn desk. "You tryin' to make trouble?"

Rick drew himself up to full height. "Of course not."

"You look like a trouble-makin' punk to me."

"Look," Rick protested, "I'm telling you the truth. She did get out. In the tunnel."

"Sure, sure." Thick, rubbery lips sneered around the mangled cigar. "She dumped you, so you gotta come in here and give me a hard time."

"Now look. I'm Rick—"

"I know who you are. I seen you and punks like you all my life." The sneer turned ugly. "You don't get outta here, I'm calling the cops and let them search those fancy pants pockets of yours. See what it is you got in there, find out how you got the money to buy them clothes." The man half rose from his chair and pointed one stubby finger at the door. "It ain't enough you gotta come around here selling your stuff. Now you wanna give me trouble? Go on, get outta here, or I'll show you what real trouble is."

Fuming with rage and embarrassment, Rick stumbled out the door and down the rotting stairs. He walked across the mushy ground lining the back sides of the tents, following the path around to where it intersected the central grounds.

The carnival was winding down. People wandered in little clusters, their gaiety sounding forced and tired, like revelers who refused to leave a party that was already over. Rick walked under the garish lights, searching for a girl he no longer believed he would find, feeling like an idiot.

The carnival manager was right, he knew it in his gut. Consuela had made a fool of him. She was probably already back in her bed, giggling into her pillow at how silly she had made him look. Three solid hours he had searched the grounds, until his third argument with the rollercoaster operator forced the harried man to send him back to the manager's office. Rick kicked angrily at an empty popcorn box, wheeled about, and headed for the exit. He had never been so humiliated in his life.

He took his anger out on the car, pushing the massive engine up to redline, taking turns in full four-wheel squeals, hitting insane speeds on the straights. It was not until he pulled into the driveway that he realized just how crazy he had been. He cut off the motor, sat in the car listening to the engine clink, and felt his anger give way to the same shaky nerves that always followed his outbursts. What if the cops had picked him up? What if his parents had been called down to the station to bail him out? What if he had wrecked and been injured, couldn't play ball, lost the scholarship, lost the good life?

The good life. That was his dad's expression. Rick sat in the car and heard the words echo through his brain. "You're destined for the good life, son. You've got it all. Looks, brains, build, backing. Just remember how lucky you are and behave. Make us proud."

Make them proud. He heard them say that endlessly, even when they didn't really say anything at all. It was with him all the time. Their expectations were constantly pushing him to strive, work, measure up, achieve.

Rick left the car and walked up the cobblestone path, climbed the wide brick stairs, passed under the tall two-story columns, unlocked the door, entered the front hall, fingered the code into the alarm system, heard the safety peep, and turned on the lights. His parents weren't back yet. They seldom were in before him on the weekends. They were local movers and shakers and were invited everywhere. Friday afternoons were times to avoid being at home. His mother was always in a whirlwind of frantic preparations, shouting orders to anyone who came within reach. His dad would rush in from work, shout back, change clothes, and then together they would put on their polished outside masks and leave.

As usual, Rick tried to make it down the domed entrance hall without giving the full-size family portrait a glance. He hated that painting. Rick stood between his seated parents, an arm on each of their shoulders, his number one fake grin firmly in place. The perfect son. Never any trouble to his folks, always tops at whatever he did, always polite around his parents' friends, always popular, always successful. Always measuring up.

His room had one wall of shelves, all filled with trophies. The maid had strict instructions to polish everything once a week, more often if they were entertaining. His dad liked to bring his cronies up, show off everything, point to the school banners he had ordered Rick to nail onto the wall—all the schools that had offered him a full scholarship. Sometimes when he had to stand there and listen to his dad boast, Rick felt as though he himself were just another trophy.

Not bothering to take off his clothes, Rick stretched out on his bed. His anger at Consuela was giving way to bafflement. Why would she go to all that trouble? Had she accepted the date just to make a fool of him? He went back over the evening in his head, but recalled nothing that might hint at sarcasm or derision. No, Consuela was not the type to make fun of somebody—at least, he didn't think so.

He checked his watch, decided it didn't matter whom he woke up, and reached for his phone. He called directory assistance, asked if there was a listing for Consuela Ortez, and struck out. She did not have her own phone. He went back downstairs, checked the directory, and found over twenty Ortez families listed, none of them living on a street that he recognized as being in Westgate. He checked his watch. After one. Too late to start calling around at random.

Rick walked back upstairs, debating which of the girls on the cheerleading squad he should call the next morning. He just needed a reason, something that would throw them off the track, and not leave them thinking that one of their friends had made him look like a fool.

The great port building gleamed silver and yellow in the night. It was utterly lacking in corners; the walls curved and flowed like great metal ribbons, one stacked upon the other, crowned by a vast circular copper dome. Balls of light suspended high overhead splashed the entire area with radiance almost as strong as day. Wander walked beside Consuela and watched her examine everything with wide-eyed wonderment. The robotaxi, the automated street cleaner, the bulbous freight carriers, the vast stretches of almost empty parking for ground cars—everything was new to her. Twice she stumbled and would have fallen save for the grip she kept on his hand, once when a hovercraft alighted, and once when a senior cargo captain passed them with a perfunctory salute. Wander saw the questions in her eyes and had a thousand questions of his own, but for the moment was content to walk alongside this remarkable girl and feel her soft hand cling to his.

The doors sighed back, and Consuela passed through, her eyes never seeming to blink. Inside, the spaceport was great open spaces and burnished marble floors and sparkling surfaces. The info-voice whispered its habitual, "Greetings and welcome to the Hegemony Spaceport. State your needs, and the way will be shown."

From the look on her face Wander realized, "You weren't even shown the spaceport?"

"No, I . . ." Consuela pointed to the triangular column rising in front of them. "Was that what spoke?"

"Scout Wander entering grounds," Wander said toward the waist-high column. Then to Consuela he said, "State your name as I did."

"Scout Consuela entering grounds," Consuela said, her voice stumbling softly over the words.

"Greetings and welcome, Scouts. Your presence is noted and Grade-C clearance granted."

"You have to say this every time you come in," Wander said. "Your voice is checked against records, and security flashes your image. Then if you don't know where to go, you speak like this." He turned back to the column and said,

"Request guidance to private quarters of Scout Consuela."

"Follow the yellow path," came the instant reply. At Wander's feet a light appeared and shot out across the hall, disappearing around a corner.

"That's great," Consuela cried, so delighted by the simple spectacle that Wander had to laugh.

He said, "Not really. It's fine when you only have a few people looking for something, but when the port is busy, the floor looks like a spider web and everybody gets mixed up. Last week we had some Hegemony bigwig get so lost we had to hold up the vessel outbound for—"

"Scout Wander, are you not on duty?"

Wander stiffened to full alert, gave an instant to hoping that his hand-holding with Consuela had been hidden by the folds of their robes, and without turning replied, "Twenty minutes still, Pilot."

"Don't leave your arrival to the last minute," snapped the reedy voice behind them. "And who, pray tell, is this?"

"Scout Consuela, sir."

"Scout who? We don't have any Scout Consuela. . . ." The tall, gaunt man stepped in front of them. He wore the midnight blue robes of a full pilot, his shoulders flecked with the stars of seniority. His head was utterly void of hair—no eyebrows, no beard, no nothing. It granted his eyes an even more piercing quality than they already had. He lifted the noteboard from its waist pouch, keyed in, then nodded. "Ah, yes. The newcomer. The name escaped me for a moment." Frosty gray eyes peered at her. "I suppose Alena checked you in?"

Consuela gave a hesitant nod. Wander winced at the coming storm, but the pilot was too miffed to notice Consuela's lack of proper reply. "I thought so," he groused. "Typical of her sloppy work. No details noted whatsoever.

I am amazed you were even outfitted. Did she manage to show you your quarters?"

"No, sir," Consuela said meekly.

"No, Pilot," he corrected automatically, his eyes still on the noteboard. "Sirs are passengers and other cattle." He shook his head. "Just look at this. She didn't even manage to note your homeworld. I would castigate her severely were she not already outbound for her new assignment. Well, that is certainly no loss." He gave an exasperated sigh. "At least this is the last mess of hers I shall have to clear up. All right. Where are you from, Scout?"

"Baltimore," came the timid reply.

"Baltimore?" A hairless brow furrowed in concentration. "That is a world unknown to me."

"I believe it is beyond the Rim, Pilot," Wander offered.

"Ah. An outworlder. Of course. There are few ships out your way, I suppose, and thus you were granted entry at this late date." He peered at her over the board, his gaze openly curious, before murmuring, "Remarkable. Well, once again talent is shown to have no borders."

"If you are busy, Pilot Grimson," Wander volunteered, "I could show her around."

"Yes, I suppose the outworld newcomer will be needing a guide. Very well, Scout, but I caution you not to shirk your other duties"—he glanced at his chronolog—"which include reporting to the duty officer immediately."

"On the bounce, Pilot," Wander replied and motioned with his head for Consuela to follow him. Once they were out of earshot, he told her, "That wasn't too bad."

"He is important?" Consuela asked.

"Senior Pilot Grimson is responsible for the scout training course," Wander replied. "And he has a reputation that reaches through the Hegemony. The first day I was on the course, my guide told me the reason you never saw scouts with more than ten downchecks on their record was that Grimson ate them for breakfast. Sometimes I almost believe it."

Consuela hesitated at the entrance to the Plexiglas chute. Grateful for the chance to take her hand once more, Wander assured her, "It's easy. Just grasp one of the rails and let it guide you up. Come on, we can take this one together, if you don't mind being a little cramped."

She shook her head, then stepped in with him, and when the gravity diminished to one-tenth G, she let out a little, "Ooooh."

He found her innocence delightful. "The first time I stepped into a gravity chute—I was only twelve or thirteen—I thought the idea was to climb. I got all tangled up with this woman in a long veil, and the only thing that saved me from serious trouble was that I screamed so loudly she was glad to let me go."

She followed his example, locking her arm into the support-rod so that her twelve-pound weight was kept stationary. She asked him, "Are you from beyond the—I forgot what he called it?"

"The Rim," he said, suddenly ashamed. "I'm sorry. Outworlder isn't a nice thing to call you. The way people say it around here, it means primitive."

"I suppose it's true," she said, looking at the grand vista of the spaceport. "Compared to this."

"I'm from right here," Wander said, for some reason feeling able to tell her anything. "The reason I had never seen a gravity chute is because there aren't any in the barrio. And I was twelve before I ever left it, except when I would come over to the field to watch the ships take off and land. That's how I got my name. From what my family says, I started wandering off as soon as I learned how to walk. There's this busy highway between the barrio and the port, but I found a drainage tunnel that was just high enough for me to walk through."

She was watching him with grave dark eyes. "You were born in a barrio?"

"The worst in the Hegemony," he stated. "My dad was a miner until he lost his leg in a phaser accident. My mom worked as a servant in a rich pilot's house. She used to tell us stories about how the man lived, but we didn't really believe her. Nobody could live like that, we thought."

Her gaze did not flinch at the shameful truth, so he asked, "What about you?"

"I never knew my father," she replied calmly, her gaze locked in on his. "My mother drinks."

He felt a sense of harmony so strong it filled his chest to bursting. "My dad hits the bottle hard too. Here we are, this is our level. Okay, step out, that's it, keep your legs loose until the gravity stabilizes, great, you've got it." He pointed to the great bronze doors. "This is the Control Tower. You can come in if you like, but I'll be pretty busy. They keep the scouts running errands and playing the mind games."

"Mind games?"

"You'll see." He pointed down a corridor behind them. "Your quarters will be along there somewhere. There's another info column just around the corner. Ask for directions. Tell your name to the door, that will give you entry. My room is thirty-four, the last on the hall. If you have any trouble, come down and state your name, and I'll code it for you to have entry. Are you hungry?"

"Yes."

"The room controls are voice coded. Say 'lights' and they'll switch on or off, whichever they are not at the moment. Same for bed, desk, chair, shower, and so on. We work odd hours, so there's a meal chute in each room. Just ask for menu. Okay?"

She squeezed his hand and dredged up a smile. "You've been really nice to me. Thank you." She hesitated, then said, "I really appreciate your sharing the spectacle with me. If I don't see you again, I just wanted you to know that."

"What do you mean? I'm your guide. We'll be seeing a lot of each other."

She remained unconvinced. "Anyway, I think you are a really nice person."

"I have watch for three hours," he said, finding it hard to get the words out. "Then I'll go to bed, unless you want to come by."

She shook her head. "I'm pretty tired."

"Sure. Oh, and one thing. Don't mention mind-lag to the pilot. He thinks a scout should be able to control things like that, and you'll get a downcheck."

"Thank you, Wander," she said quietly, and something in her voice made it sound as though she were saying good-bye.

"You're welcome," he replied, unable to mask his grin. "If you like, I'll come by and collect you for class."

Again there was the hesitation, then, "That would be fine. Good-night."

He watched her make her way down the hallway, pausing to take in everything from the view out over the ship fields to the circular illumination-sculpture poised near the ceiling. Wander had the momentary impression that she was trying to imprint it all on her memory, as though seeing it for the first and last time. Then he shook his head. Mind-lag did strange things to people. In his few weeks here, he had already heard a number of travelers' stories.

He turned and announced himself to the security doors, then bounded up the curving ramp leading to the tower, a sense of gaiety leaving him weightless.

–FOUR–

Consuela lay in the darkness that had been her most secret shield for as long as she could remember. Her tiny room was a sort of afterthought, placed in the exact center of the tenement apartment, and had no windows. When she was little, she would retreat from the bad times by coming in and turning off the lights and sliding under her bed. With her cheek pressed against the cold hardwood floor and her arms cuddling the blanket's scratchy warmth, she would give herself over to dreams. Then one day when she was nine, Consuela bumped her head and the dreams became real. Sort of. For a while.

Now she was older, and reality did not scare her as it once had. The loneliness she had known as a child still remained her constant companion, but she was no longer frightened. Now she knew she possessed an inner strength that would help her through the toughest trials. As she had grown up, she had also grown determined.

Consuela saved every cent she made toward college. She was going to study computer software and graphic design. She had read that this was the coming wave and that companies could not find enough qualified people. Salaries were good, and work was plentiful. That was why she was so set on college, to find a good job. At the ripe old age of seventeen, Consuela had already gained enough experience of poverty and hardship to last a lifetime.

She had almost succeeded in putting the experiences shared with her friends Daniel and Bliss behind her. They were almost relegated to the realm of a little girl's daydreams. But as she lay in the darkness of her closet-room, the slender line of light blocked from coming in under her door by the rug she always jammed in place before lying down, Consuela found herself reluctant to let this particular memory go.

She knew what she had witnessed out there on the frozen field was more than just a dream. The whole experience had been too vivid and too real to have been imagined. And Wander. She rolled over, hugging her pillow to her chest. He had the saddest eyes she had ever seen. She would remember those eyes for a very long time to come.

She did not know why these experiences came specifically to her, but come they had, and the purpose behind them was a lot clearer this morning than it had been when she was nine. They were lessons, she understood that now. And this lesson had been given to her by Wander, when he had held himself there beside her in the chute and said with that calm sorrowful strength of his that he had been born in a barrio.

Consuela sighed long and deeply, wishing there were some way to have spent more time with him. In Wander she had felt a kinship, a bonding that went beyond time and space and the borders of dreams. She had sensed a depth that mirrored her own, a harmony of hearts. Yes, she would go out and live the lesson, but now there would be another secret never to be shared. She would tell the world who she was and where she came from, but never would she reveal the beautiful secret of Wander's eyes.

Sally. As Consuela sat up and swung her feet to the floor, she decided that the first person she should tell was her best friend, Sally. At least Sally would not laugh at her.

Then her feet touched the floor, and Consuela cried aloud.

Instead of a scuffed hardwood floor, she felt soft carpet. She reached out, moving blindly until she touched the wall, and cried again. The warm-smooth surface tingled slightly under her fingers, as though the power required to produce the articles upon demand could be felt.

"Light!" she gasped, and cried a third time when the illumination revealed the alien room, her pale blue robe lying crumpled on the floor where she had flung it.

"Bed!" Silently her bed retreated back into the wall, melding into the bland, smooth surface. Now the room was utterly bare, save for a small plaque by the door. There were listed, in a strange language which somehow she could read perfectly well, all the commands that the room understood.

"Mirror!" she called, and when the reflecting surface was revealed, Consuela stared into the sleep-tousled face of a scared young woman.

The doorchime caused her to leap completely clear of the floor. A disembodied voice announced calmly, "Scout Wander requests entry."

"Just a minute." Frantically she plucked up the robe and slipped it on, grasped the long feather-light stocking-boots and pulled them up. She moved back to the mirror, brushed her hair with her fingers, then straightened, took a deep breath, and said, "Door."

Wander was there, smiling in such a way that even the usual sadness of his eyes was muted. The sight of him touched her so unexpectedly that she had a sudden urge to rush up and hug him close. Instead she smiled and said, "I'm still here."

"So I see. Mind-lag better?"

"I think so."

"Excellent. Have you eaten?"

"Not yet." Wanting him to know how great it was to see him again, she said, "I was sort of waiting for you."

A flush of pleasure crept out of his collar and spread across his features. "We'd better hurry, then. Class starts in less than an hour."

Sally was totally astonished, when her mother called her downstairs Saturday morning, to greet Rick at her front door.

He stood there looking foolish, trying to hide it behind a big smile. "Hey, Sals, how's it going?"

"Rick!" She pulled her overlong T-shirt down straight and wished she could slam the door, shout at her mother for not giving her fair warning, and race back upstairs for makeup and other clothes. "What are you doing here? I mean, would you like to come in?"

"No thanks. Look, I'm sorry to come by so early, but I talked to Cindy this morning, and she said you might know where Consuela lived." Cindy was head cheerleader and girlfriend of Rick's best buddy. "She said Consuela gave her some story about their redoing the exchanges in her neighborhood or something, she wasn't sure. Anyway, she didn't even have her telephone number."

"I don't either," Sally said, both relieved and jealous that the reason for Rick's visit was Consuela and not her. What was it about that girl? "I kept asking her for it, and she always gave me one excuse or another. I guess I finally just gave up."

Rick looked skeptical. "You're her best friend, and you don't have her number?"

"I know it sounds crazy, but Consuela is real mysterious about a lot of stuff." Sally shrugged. "I don't even know where she lives."

"But her telephone number? Come on, you've got to be kidding."

"I don't have it. Really. Why, is something the matter?"

Instantly Rick's attitude became overly casual. "No, of course not. We just had a sort of crazy end to the night, you know, and I wanted to talk with her. That's all."

They had a fight. Sally could not totally hide her smirk. He tried to put the moves on her, and Consuela gave him the brush-off. Way to go, girl. "Gee, I wish I could help, Rick. But unless Consuela calls me, I've got to wait and see her at school."

"Hey, it's no big deal. I'll talk to her Monday." Another of the patented Rick smiles. "Have a great weekend, okay?"

"Thanks, Rick. You too."

"If you hear from her, ask her to give me a call." He skipped lightly down the stairs and walked toward his car. "See you around."

–FIVE–

It was all his fault.

Wander did not mean to make their arrival so late. But talking was so easy with Consuela. At breakfast he lost all track of time, until he happened to look up and realize they were the only scouts left in the residents' hall. He glanced at the wall chrono and leapt to his feet. "Come on!"

"What's the matter?"

"Class is starting right now. Hurry!"

Together they raced down the corridors and entered the room just as Pilot Grimson stepped onto the podium. Bad, but no downcheck.

The pilot frowned in their direction. "You are setting what unfortunately is coming to be the expected example from you, Scout Wander." He silenced the snickers that rose from the room with a single frigid glare, then turned his attention back to the pair. "Scout Consuela, I will expect you to appear more promptly from now on."

"Yes, Pilot," she said quietly.

"Very well. You will take the seat corresponding to your chamber number. This will apply to all training rooms and lecture halls." As Consuela walked to where he pointed,

Grimson continued to the class as a whole, "I ask you to join me in welcoming the newest addition to this scout squadron. Consuela's arrival was unavoidably delayed by a lack of transport to the Hegemony."

From beside the podium, Wander heard the boy seated next to Consuela's station mutter, "Another outworlder." He felt great shame for her until he saw her settle into her place, turn, and fasten the boy with a fathomless gaze. The boy held it for a moment, then wilted.

Wander turned back to the podium and felt his pleasure mount when he saw Pilot Grimson's thin lips curve into a small smile of approval. Wander cleared his throat and said quietly, "Pilot, I believe—"

"Your place awaits you, Scout Wander," the pilot replied coldly. "If you have business with me, I suggest you arrive before the entire class has gathered."

Wander knew he was taking his life in his hands, but he had to try. "Pilot, if you please—"

Grimson swiveled, looked down from the dais, and froze Wander with his glare. The scout had no choice but to retreat to his seat.

"Now then," Pilot Grimson said, his scowl following Wander into his seat before dropping to the podium's controls. "Today we begin the second phase of your training. As many of you have already surmised, the first three weeks have primarily been a time of culling. It is not enough for you to have talent. You must also have the ability to direct, to focus, to orient both yourselves and the ships that will one day be placed under your care."

Wander sensed the electric change in the room. Spines stiffened, bodies leaned forward in anticipation. They had made it. Over two-thirds of those who originally entered the scout squadron were gone. But the culling was over. Port scuttlebutt had predicted this would happen. A point was reached when each scout squadron was deemed ready. Those remaining were the ones not only sensitive to the higher energies, but able to *use* them.

From this point on, they were almost assured of a position. Some would become port communications officers, directing incoming and outgoing ships. Others would be assigned permanent duty as interstellar communicators, manning stations throughout the Hegemony and beyond the Rim. Others with greater clarity might act as backup navigators. Some would escort passenger vessels flying the permanently channeled inner-Hegemony spaceways. A few might have the abilities required to direct the flight of long-distance freighters. And perhaps one candidate in three or four squadrons might have the abilities required to rise to the highest honor of all—Senior Pilot, Navigator to Starfleet Command.

"All of you have demonstrated the ability to draw upon the power placed at your disposal and identify what remains unseen to the physical eye," Grimson droned on, watching his panel lights flicker to green as the hall's amplifiers reached full power. "Now begins the process of learning control. You must learn to override the physical senses and focus entirely upon the data being obtained through your headsets. You must set aside all distractions, all random thoughts, all outside sensations, and *focus*."

He scanned each eager face in turn, then nodded. "Very well. Attach your headsets and connect."

Wander watched as Consuela grappled with the unfamiliar equipment. When she finally looked his way, he raised his own headset and slid it around his forehead like a padded headband, fitting the two cushioned points to his temples. She followed his example and gave a smile of thanks. He pointed to the single black switch set to the right of the writing pad and thumbed it to the "on" position, but when she did the same, he felt a rising sense of alarm. He reached under his desk and fingered the override switch, which only his desk had. As he did so, he hoped fervently that his premonition was wrong. And just as strongly hoped that he was right.

"For the next few days," Pilot Grimson continued, "there will be no downcheck given to anyone who wishes to withdraw from the lesson. If you feel yourself losing touch, withdraw, re-orient, then continue. Therefore it is suggested that you rest your hand near the power switch. I urge you, however, not to retreat unless absolutely necessary. Five days from now, when we enter our first simulation exercise, you will be downchecked for retreating."

He checked the controls set in the curved podium and went on, "Today you will be expected to find your way through a maze, charting your course on paper. This means that you will no longer be able to keep your eyes closed at all times. You must begin to learn to see visually while focusing. Marks will be given both for finding the quickest route to the goal, and for doing so in the shortest amount of time."

Grimson flickered a glance toward Wander, who understood perfectly. He was not to be the first to finish. Wander swallowed his qualms over Consuela and replied with a minute nod.

"One important clue," Pilot Grimson offered. "It is possible to reorient your perspective and see the entire maze from above, but only if you are able to reach beyond the perspective of barriers and first identify the goal."

Wander risked a glance around the chamber. The squadron's study hall was a domed structure, shaped like a broad shell, with curving half-rings of tables rising up before the pilot's dais. Wander saw many confused looks among the forty or so scouts. He knew a moment's sympathy.

Up to now, their most difficult task had been to correctly identify some item that was not visible with the physical eye. Now they were to be presented with a maze that they could not even see, and not only were they expected to find their way through it but to identify the goal before they started. Wander understood the purpose behind this task, but knew that few others would be able to. A pilot was required to focus upon both the starting point and the destination at all times. It was only when both were held in tandem that a safe interstellar transport was possible.

"Are there any questions?" The class had by now learned that the offer was symbolic and obediently remained silent. "Very well." Pilot Grimson reached down and began coding in. "Prepare for vision. I will begin the countdown from five, four, three, two, one."

Instantly the silence was shattered by a bloodcurdling scream.

Before he was even consciously aware that he had moved, Wander was on his feet and tearing off his headset. Consuela fell writhing to the floor, shrieking so loudly the student beside her toppled from his chair. Wander fought his way around the circle, shoving other scouts out of the way.

"Make it stop! Make it stop!" Consuela screamed. Wander leapt over the student's frozen prostrate form and ripped the headset from Consuela's head. She gave a final cry, whimpered, and fainted in his arms.

Pilot Grimson tumbled down beside him. He pressed two fingers into the pulse-point at the base of her chin, concentrated, then permitted his shoulders to slump slightly in relief. But not for long. Swiftly he collected himself and rose to full height. "I want to know who did this," he said, his voice an ice-bladed knife. "I *demand* to know who sabotaged this scout's controls."

The class remained frozen in gaping silence. Wander struggled to his feet, holding Consuela's limp form in his arms.

"Can you manage?" Grimson asked.

"Yes, Pilot." He could not stop his voice from trembling. It was all his fault.

"Straighten up," Grimson snapped. He turned back to the room. "Very well. If the culprit refuses to give himself up, you may all consider yourselves downchecked. You will remain here until I have returned, and you will remain *silent*." He wheeled about. "Come with me, Scout."

Wander followed the pilot from the room. Once they were outside and the door closed, Grimson hustled down the hall. "To the infirmary. Quickly. Do you wish me to help?"

"No thank you, Pilot. She's not so heavy." And it was his fault. He could not release her.

"Did you suspect this?"

"Yes, Pilot."

"And was this what you wished to tell me about?"

"Yes, Pilot."

His hairless face blazed with cold fury. "Your habitual tardiness has almost cost us the life of a Talent."

"Yes, Pilot, I know." Wander's misery could not have been greater.

Grimson keyed the infirmary door, snapped for lights, then helped Wander settle Consuela's inert form on the padded stretcher. Harshly he ordered the communicator to locate the duty medic and send him up on the bounce. He checked her pulse once more, peeled back one eyelid, seemed relieved to hear her moan.

When the white-robed medic popped through the door,

the pilot growled, "What took you so long?"

"Pilot, I—"

"Never mind. This girl has suffered an extreme amplified mental shock. For the record, someone tampered with her headset."

The medic's eyes widened to round moons. "A Talent?"

Grimson hesitated, then nodded. "Perhaps. But you are ordered to keep it under your hat. We have not yet confirmed anything."

"Yes, Pilot, I understand."

"I want a report as quickly as possible. You will find me in the squadron's training hall." Pilot Grimson motioned toward the door. "Come with me, Scout."

The infirmary door sighed shut behind them. Wander felt hollowed and weak, capable only of the thought that it was all his fault.

The pilot finally said, "I see that you are punishing yourself far better than I ever could."

Wander swallowed. "Do you think she's all right?"

"You suffered a similar shock, if my memory of your records is correct."

"When I was eleven."

"Then you know what she is feeling, and what will happen when she awakens." His tone was surprisingly mild. "Tell me why you suspected her abilities."

"Last night we watched a transport launch together."

"Where?"

"Beside the reservoir." Wander could not take his eyes from the door. "I think she could hear the countdown with me."

There was a long silence, then, "Look at me, Scout."

Wander tore his eyes away, looked into Pilot Grimson's penetrating gaze. The man searched his face for a long time, as though seeking something only he could see, before asking, "You can follow ship communications without amplification?"

Wander started, realizing he had finally let go of his long-held secret. Then he decided it really did not matter, not with Consuela unconscious inside the infirmary. It was all his fault. "Yes, Pilot."

"Without amplification?"

"Yes, Pilot." The man's eerily soft voice helped him focus. "But not through a shielded structure like the port. I have to be outside somewhere."

The hairless face inched closer. A trace of the customary coldness returned to his voice. "You had best not be trying to trick me, boy."

"I've been going out there and watching ships depart and following them in my mind since I was five years old," Wander said, not caring anymore. All the years of scorn and derision, all the shouts of laughter when as a child he would respond to voices only he could hear. The punishments, the scoldings, the accusations by teachers and family that he was imagining, lying, insane, that he was a troubled little boy. All the anger came rushing to the surface. "It's all I know," he said, his voice as hot as his face. "It's all I've ever done."

Surprisingly, the pilot seemed unfazed by Wander's outburst. "Your record mentioned this ability when you were young. It is rare, but not unheard of, in children. I recall seeing no indication of this in your later tests, however."

"I lied," Wander replied flatly.

"I see," Pilot Grimson said slowly, then straightened. The gray eyes showed no reaction whatsoever, they just continued to hold him fast. "Can you hear Control Tower from here?"

"Whispers," Wander replied. "The tower doors are shielded. I hear the whispers all the time. If I concentrate,

I can make out the individual voices. But I try not to. It's hard enough when I'm on duty."

"Why haven't you told me this before?"

"I haven't heard of anyone else being able to hear like this. I know the others can't. The highborns give me a hard enough time as it is." Wander took a breath. "And to be honest, Pilot, I'm scared of you."

"And well you should be," the man replied, but without menace. "So how do you work on tower duty?"

"I stole a training headset," Wander replied, glad to have it all out in the open. "My father was a miner. I cut strips from his lead-lined protective garment and pasted it to the headset. With my temples partially covered and the band across my forehead the noise is cut down to a level I can stand."

"I see," the pilot said again. "Did you know there is an attachment available to Tower amps called a desensitizer?"

It was Wander's turn to stare. Slowly he shook his head. So there were others. There were others *like him*.

"No, of course not. But had you not been so secretive, you might have saved yourself and the young lady inside a great deal of distress."

The infirmary door slid back. "She appears to be okay," the medic announced. "All vital signs check out. I've given her something, and she's resting peacefully. But if she's a Talent, you know how disoriented she's going to be when she wakes up."

"Thank you, Medic," the pilot said, and stopped Wander's forward motion with one upraised finger. "We will join you momentarily."

"Yes, Pilot." The medic stepped back, and the infirmary door slid shut behind him.

"Very well, Scout. I want you to remain by Scout Consuela's side until she is fully recovered." A glint of frosty humor surfaced in those probing gray eyes. "I assume that will not be too harsh a duty."

"No, Pilot. Thank you."

"We will discuss all this further once the incident is behind us. For now, I have a class I must see to." Grimson granted him a slight nod before striding down the hall.

Wander turned back to the infirmary and called the door open. His heart twisted at the sight of Consuela's pale form. The medic stood and dropped his magazine. "You been assigned watch over the patient?"

"Yes."

He walked to the door, then turned and smirked down at the sleeping girl. "Pity those looks have got to be wasted on a Talent."

"They're not wasted," Wander replied.

"She'll end up locked up like all the others," the medic told him. "A waste, just like I said."

Wander raised his gaze. "Like what others?"

Suddenly the medic realized with whom he was talking, and his smirk slipped a notch. "Just rumors, Scout."

"You know something," Wander insisted. "Tell me."

Consuela chose that moment to moan softly. "Better see to your patient, Scout." The medic sidled toward the door. "That's a lot more important than bandying rumors about."

Wander waited until the door had slid shut, then took Consuela's hand. Her hair looked impossibly dark, strewn as it was across the white covering. Wander tucked the blanket around her shoulders, then sat back, his gaze fixed upon her face, and gave himself over to memories of the past and yearnings for the future.

–Six–

When Consuela did not show up for school on Monday, Rick could calm himself no longer with vague hopings that all was as it should be. One minute he was angry with her for making a fool of him. The next he was worried that something really bad might have happened. One minute more and he was completely baffled.

He stopped by the principal's office before lunch and used charm by the bucketful on the school secretary. By the time he was finished, the poor woman no longer knew whether she was coming or going. She made not a whimper of protest as he scribbled down Consuela's home address from her permanent records.

After football practice he drove straight to the Westgate subdivision. But the first three people he stopped had never heard of Loden Boulevard. Then one old geezer out walking his dog told him, "Sure I know Loden. But you won't find it in Westgate."

"That's where my friend said she lived."

"Then either your friend is lying or she don't know the name of her street," the old guy said, stooping down to quiet his dog. "I've lived in these parts all my life, and the only Loden in Baltimore runs right smack dab through the middle of Sutton Park."

Rick reached over and turned off the engine. In the sudden silence he felt things falling into place. Sutton Park was one of the city's worst neighborhoods. It bordered on Westgate, and the locals were always after the city to either clean the place up or tear it down. Yes, it was making sense.

He turned back to the old man, who was watching him with a shrewd gaze. "Girl made herself out to be something more than she was, did she?"

Rick found himself unable to let that one pass. "She's one of the finest people I've ever met."

"Then you better grab hold, sonny," the old man replied, not in the least put out. "Anybody who can pull themselves outta Sutton is a prize. She pretty?"

"Yes," Rick said, his face growing hot. "She is."

"That'll have made it all the more hard for the young lady." The old man nodded sagely. "Yessir, if I was the one driving that fancy car, I'd make a beeline over to that gal's house and put a padlock on her heart."

"How do I get there, please?"

"Turn yourself around and head down this very road about a mile to the first major intersection. That's where Westgate ends. Go through that light, and your next road is Loden. You got a street number?"

"Twelve seventeen."

"Then you'll want to go right. It's bad up there, but not as bad as it is down southward." The old geezer grinned at him and patted the Corvette's roof. "Gal from those parts, she's gonna think you're her knight in shining armor."

Rick found the street and paid to park his car in a guarded lot, which was a lot cheaper than having to buy a new radio, side window, and four new tires with rims. He walked the cracked and buckling sidewalk past tawdry shops with barred windows and loud rap music thumping through open doors. It seemed as if every corner had a liquor store. The people were a mixture of white and black and Latino and Asian. His height and his clean-cut features and his nice clothes earned him a lot of looks, none of them kind. Rick picked up his pace almost to a trot, counting off those house numbers he could spot, and vowed to be out of the area before nightfall.

The stairs leading to Consuela's front door were crumbling, and the rusting bank of doorbells had a spaghetti of disconnected wires dangling from their base. The old door complained loudly as he pulled it open. He walked across the broken mosaic floor and pushed through canted inner doors, their broken windowpanes repaired with cardboard and masking tape. The inner hall stank of old refuse and rang with the sounds of screaming children and blaring televisions. The walls were mildewed, and the only light was a bare bulb hanging high overhead. Rick checked the paper in his hand, then started for the stairs.

The woman who answered his knock was no doubt once very beautiful, but now her features were as blurred as her voice and her eyes. "Yeah? Whaddaya want?"

Rick was not used to speaking to somebody through a cracked door with two chains holding it from opening farther. "Mrs. Ortez?"

"The name's Johnson. Who're you?"

"Oh, I'm sorry. I was looking for the apartment of Consuela Ortez."

The woman made an effort to focus. "Consuela's sick. I called you people this morning. How come you can't just leave us alone?"

Rick stared. "You're Consuela's mother?"

"Why do I have to go through this every time you assign someone new?" Her voice rose to a habitual whine. "My husband was Puerto Rican. He left us soon after Consuela was born, and I've never heard from him since. Consuela has his last name on her birth certificate. I changed my name back. It's all legal and down in black and white, if you'd just take time to check your records."

"I'm not from the school, Mrs. Johnson. I'm a friend of Consuela's. May I speak with her, please?"

Watery green eyes squinted in concentration. "You sure you're not from the office?"

"I'm just a friend, honest. We had a date Friday and, well, to be honest, I'm not exactly sure what happened. I'd just like to talk with her and make sure everything's okay."

Mrs. Johnson tucked strands of grayish blond hair back into her unkempt bun. Rick saw that her fingers were red and chapped raw, the fingernails bitten to the quick. "Well, if you're sure you're her friend."

"Really, Mrs. Johnson. Please."

"Just a minute." The door closed, and he heard chains being ratcheted back. The door opened once more to admit him as the woman backed up on unsteady legs. "You're really her friend?"

Rick nodded, trying hard not to stare around the threadbare room. From the woman's unkempt appearance, he guessed Consuela was the one responsible for the place being so clean. But nothing could hide the poverty. "Yes, ma'am. Could I speak with her, please? I won't be a minute."

"She's not here," she replied, and for the first time a hint of worry showed through. "She hasn't been home since Friday night."

"What?" Rick felt his knees grow weak.

"She went off to see some friends. I think that's what she said. Something about bowling."

"She had a date with me, Mrs. Johnson."

"She didn't say anything about a date," her mother re-plied, more certain about that than anything since opening the door. "It was a couple of girlfriends. But I can't remem-ber their names. My memory is a mess."

Rick felt insulted. Why would she not want her mother to know she had a date with him? "Could I maybe check her room? Maybe there's something there you missed."

Mrs. Johnson hesitated, then said, "I suppose it's all right. First door down the hall. You're sure you're not from the office?"

"Just a friend." Rick crossed the living room and en-tered the stubby hallway. The first door opened into a cramped windowless room. It was utterly spotless. Every-thing had its place, a place for everything. The bed was neatly made, the few books stacked along shelves made from raw planks and concrete blocks. The walls were cov-ered with advertisements for past orchestral performances and ballet and art exhibits. At the corner of each were tagged single tickets. Rick glanced at the books. Most were classics—Shakespeare, Milton, Thoreau, Conrad, Joyce—and all were dog-eared from heavy use. Several had their bindings taped to keep the books from falling apart. For some reason, seeing those books made him feel ashamed.

As he searched her room for something, anything, that might suggest where she had gone, Rick found himself thinking back to the year before, and the girl who had dumped him, and what she had said. He shook his head, trying to drive away the memories, but they would not go. The recollections added a frantic note to his search.

A flake. That was what Audrie had called him. A total flake. A year later, the words remained etched in his brain.

She had been a senior and a cheerleader, he the first guy ever to be made captain of the football team his junior year. The year's difference in age had been a challenge to him and a joke to her. It had been far more than puppy love, at least to him. After dating a month, she had wanted nothing to do with him. But the harder she pushed him away, the more he wanted her.

Finally she had taken him aside and talked down to him. To *him*. As if he were some unruly little brother who had to be shown his place. "I won't go out with you anymore because you're a flake," she had told him bluntly, "and with your looks there's a good chance you'll make it all the way through school without ever having to grow up."

Rick had been so stunned by the words that it was only when his anger boiled over that he could speak at all. "You're crazy. You just wish you had it so good."

Her reply had been as curt as her tone. "I don't know if I can put it in words of one syllable, and even if I could, I doubt if you would listen. Someday something is really going to shake your world and force you to grow up. I only hope it won't be too long in coming."

All Rick could think of as he searched Consuela's room was, what if the time had come? What if this was what would shake his world? The darkness of unknown dangers rattled him to his core. But try as he might, he could come up with nothing that suggested where Consuela might be.

Her homework for Monday was laid out beside her books. The only other thing on her desk was a framed portrait of a smiling younger Consuela standing between a strong-jawed man with dark hair and a beautiful blond woman. He picked up the picture and walked back out to the living room. Mrs. Johnson was seated at the dining table with a glass in her hand.

He thrust the picture forward and asked, "Can you tell me who they are?"

"Huh?" Her head moved like a puppet on a loose string.

"These two people in the photograph," Rick insisted. "Who are they?"

She struggled to focus. "Oh. Danny is a good boy. A real gent. Connie smiled a lot more when he was around."

"They've gone?"

She nodded, a bumpy motion that took her chin almost to her chest. "Out west somewhere. Chicago, maybe. Say, you want something to drink?"

"No thanks," he said, raising his voice impatiently. "Do you have their address?"

"Nope." She pointed vaguely in the kitchen's direction. "Number's on the wall by the phone."

Rick hesitated, then said, "I think maybe we better call the police, Mrs. Johnson."

That brought her around. Raw fear appeared in her eyes. "Don't," she pleaded. "They're always making trouble for me. Don't tell them she's not here."

"But Mrs. Johnson—"

"You're her friend," she begged. "You find her. Call Danny. Maybe she's there. Yeah, that's it. She's gone to visit Danny. She was always talking about it. You just call the number on the wall. Everything will work out fine."

−Seven−

It was almost eleven o'clock when the plane from Chicago landed at Baltimore International. Rick recognized the young man passing through the gate from Consuela's picture, and walked forward to meet him. Rick was growing weary, but still tried hard to put on a good face. "Hey, Dan. How's it going?"

"Rick?" The dark-haired young man wore an overcoat over his suit and a very tired expression. "Nice to meet you."

"I still can't believe you'd hop on a plane like this," Rick said. "Especially after what I told you on the phone."

"Where's your car?"

"Out front."

"Let's go." Despite his evident fatigue, Daniel set a rapid pace. "Do you think the carnival's still open?"

"Hey," Rick said, slowing down. "You're not—"

Daniel grasped his arm and urged him forward. "I know all this must be hard for you to accept. Believe me, I know. But we won't know anything for certain until we've checked it out."

"Then, you believe me?"

"Let's just say," Daniel replied, hustling through the main entrance, "I'm sympathetic to what you've been going through."

When they had piled into Rick's Corvette, Daniel slipped off his overcoat. A glint of something shiny caught Rick's eye. As he started the car, Rick studied the small, gold fish pinned to Daniel's lapel. "You really want to go to the carnival?"

Daniel nodded. "Run through the story one more time, all right?"

Rick did so, feeling the affair become more real as someone finally took him seriously. "I searched all over the place, spent almost three hours looking. Believe me, I did everything but climb back into the tunnel."

"I believe you," Daniel said quietly.

When they pulled into the carnival parking lot, Daniel was up and running even before Rick cut off the motor. Rick raced to catch up with him and demanded, "What's the hurry?"

"We need to catch the roller coaster before it stops for the night," Daniel said. "Which way?"

"Down there. But the coaster's moving too fast for you to see anything."

Daniel did not bother to reply. He ran down the gaudy thoroughfare, his streaming overcoat and tie attracting stares from the remaining fun-seekers. He bought two coaster tickets, then motioned for Rick to join him in the line. He reached into his coat, brought out a pen and a piece of paper. He scribbled hastily, then handed it to Rick. "If something happens and I don't come out, call this number in Chicago. It's my home. My wife's name is Bliss. Tell her what happened."

Rick stared at him. "What do you mean, if something happens?"

Impatiently Daniel waved it aside. "She knows why I'm here. If she decides to come down, take her on the ride too, okay?"

"What are you talking about?"

Daniel gave him a stare so grim and hard that Rick felt his protests dry up. "Listen to what I am saying. Bliss may decide she wants to come, rather than wait for me to return. If she's uncertain, tell her I said to wait. But it's her decision. If she comes, take her on the ride. All right?"

"Sure," Rick replied numbly. "But what could happen?"

"Probably nothing."

"Hey!" The barker brusquely waved them forward. "You jokers want to ride, get a move on! I ain't got all night."

Together they moved forward and allowed themselves to be seated. When the bar crashed down, Daniel settled back and sighed, "Here we go again."

Rick's query was cut short by the horn sounding, announcing that the ride was pulling out. The climb to the top seemed endless, the swoop downward uninteresting. Rick sat beside a grim-faced Daniel, allowing himself to be thrown back and forth by the centrifugal force, wondering what the guy had been talking about, wishing he could just make it all go away.

Somehow the tunnel ride felt as though it lasted a lot longer than the first time. Rick decided it was just nerves, especially when the light reappeared and he glanced to his left, and Daniel was still there. The feeling of relief was so strong he had to laugh.

But Daniel remained thoughtfully silent as they stepped from the car. He pulled Rick back around to the front and said, "Wait here." Then he stepped forward and bought another ticket. When he returned, he was pulling pen and paper from his pocket once more. "You need to write out a little note to your folks. Tell them you're going to be away for a couple of days. Make up some reason so they won't worry. Or at least, not worry too much."

Rick could scarcely believe what he was hearing. "Are you crazy?"

"Hurry, there's not much time." Daniel gave him an assessing gaze. "This isn't my trip. You need to go yourself. Alone."

"Go where?"

"Look, do you want to find Consuela, or don't you?"

"Sure, but—"

"Then every second counts. Write out the note and put your address on this second page. I'll drop your car and the note off, then catch a cab back to the airport." When Rick still did not move, Daniel leaned forward and said forcefully, "I can't do this, Rick. If you want to help Consuela you've got to believe me and do what I say."

Feeling cut off from the garish sights and sounds that surrounded him, Rick did as he was urged. When he handed back the scribbled message, Daniel read it and grunted, "It will have to do." He grasped Rick's hand, guided him forward, and said as they walked, "Will you take some advice?"

"I guess so, but—"

"When you find yourself growing lost or confused, search out the light that remains unseen. Remember that the answer does not lie in strength or power or anger, but in love. Open yourself up to His higher call, and know that you will always be protected."

Daniel patted his shoulder and handed the barker the single ticket. As Rick climbed into the seat, Daniel called out from behind the wire barrier, "Tell Consuela that when Bliss and I got married, we tried to have the court grant us custody until her mom went through a rehabilitation program. We never told her because the lawyer said it probably wouldn't work out. I've never been sure we were right to keep it quiet. Tell her we love her, and that she always has a home."

The horn sounded, the coaster started off, and Daniel shouted, "Go with God, Rick. We'll be praying for your safe return."

–Eight–

Consuela awoke with a gasping exclamation that sounded as if it had been torn from her throat. Wander squeezed her hand, pressed another upon the soft skin where neck joined shoulder, and soothed, "Easy, easy. It's going to be all right."

"Ooooh, my head. Everything keeps spinning around," she said, her voice barely a whisper.

"You've had a psychic shock." Wander's voice was calm despite his racing pulse. "Your amplifier was tuned up too high."

"Wander? Is that really you?" She struggled to open her eyes, but they swam unfocused until she groaned and closed them once more.

"It's me," he said softly.

"I'm still here," she murmured.

He had to smile. "Why do you keep saying that?"

"Don't leave me, okay? Don't let go. I feel like I'd go spinning out of control if you didn't keep hold."

"I'm here," he said quietly, daring to stroke the tiny thread of hair falling before her ear. "I'm right here."

"What happened? I know you told me already, but I don't think I understand."

"Let me tell you a story," he replied quietly. "You just lie there. It's better if you're quiet."

"Lights," she said softly. "They keep flashing in my head."

"I know. It will pass," he quietly assured her. "Listen. When I was eleven, a specialist came to my school. He was some big doctor, volunteering time to work with the barrio kids. All the teachers made a big fuss over him. They made me go see him. The doctor inspected me and said, 'There's nothing wrong with this child except he hasn't had enough to eat.' The head teacher prodded me in the shoulder and said, 'Tell the good doctor about your voices.' I will never forget how ashamed I was. I couldn't look at the doctor after that, even when he ordered me to.

"When I wouldn't say anything, the head teacher started telling him stories. About how when I was younger I would go off into these spells—that's what she called them, spells. One minute I was there, the next I wasn't. I just drifted off and away, then I would snap back and have no recollection of where I was or how I got there or why the teacher was shouting at me and why the kids were laughing."

Wander leaned back in his chair, drawing her hand closer to the edge of the bed so that he could hold it with both of his. "She told him how sometimes I would answer voices that no one else could hear, or ask questions that made no sense, or speak words that no barrio child had any way of knowing, like gravity shield release, or transition approach, or thruster station. She made me stand there while she told him how, when the kids kept laughing at me, I stopped talking about the voices. How I stopped talking at all. How for over a year I did not speak to anyone. But how I would sometimes still have these spells. And how other kids would talk about how I spent all my free time wandering around the port, sitting for hours in the haunted fields that everyone else refused to walk through.

"I had to keep standing there, terrified that all my secrets were coming out. I knew they were going to do something to me. I just knew it. I stood there and tried to shut out her voice and wished the floor would just open up and swallow me whole."

Slowly, gradually, inch by inch, Consuela turned her head. She opened one eye at a time, her brow furrowed with the effort of trying to focus on Wander. When both of those beautiful dark eyes were fastened on his face, he asked, "Feeling any better?"

"I think so. This will really go away?"

"Yes. Are you thirsty?"

"Very."

When he brought the cup over, she opened her mouth, accepted the straw and swallowed, holding her head as still as she could. "Thank you."

Wander settled back and went on, "The doctor made the head teacher leave the room. He then took hold of my shoulders and guided me over to a seat and forced me to sit down. I can still remember how his hands smelled, clean and a little soapy. He had a very deep voice. He told me that he was going to sit there for as long as it took for me to stop being shy and speak with him. But until I was ready, he was going to talk, because he didn't like wasting time. He was not a volunteer as the school thought. He was paid by the Hegemony. There, he said, he had told me a secret. One he knew a silent boy like me would keep. But he hoped that because he had been so honest and open with me, I would think about talking to him.

"Then he said that his job was to look for sensitives, had I ever heard that word? When I did not answer, he told me that there were different stages, and almost everyone was at least a little sensitive. But for reasons no one could explain, some people had more sensitivity than others. A lot more. These people were called Talents. And one of the first signals of a Talent child was that they heard voices."

Wander stopped, stroked her arm, and said, "Am I boring you?"

"No," she said softly. "Go on."

"How do you feel?"

"Better. The spinning isn't so bad. Go on."

"All right. The doctor asked me, did I ever hear the voices talk about countdowns?" Wander smiled at the memory. "I could scarcely believe my ears. Here was somebody who not only did not laugh at me but knew what I was hearing. I raised my head, and this seemed to please him very much. He asked me, 'Can you remember what the pilot says when he starts his own counting?' And I said, very quietly, 'Two minutes.' The doctor became extremely excited, and it scared me, but not too much, because somehow I got the impression that he was also very pleased. He had trouble opening his case, his hands were trembling so bad. He pulled out this steel-backed pad that had a questionnaire attached to it. He scribbled something across the top, and then looked back at me. I remember his hair was almost as dark as yours, but his eyes were pale blue. He had a mustache and thick, dark hair on the back of his hands. I remember the room smelled dusty, and there was sunlight coming in though the window. I remember that day as clearly as this one. I will never forget it. Never. My life started on that day."

Wander felt he was looking into two worlds at the same time. The one before him was filled with the beauty of Consuela's open gaze. The other was the one in his mind, made more real than ever before by the chance to share it with someone. "Then he asked me, 'What is the word for the opening a starship passes through?' and I said in my very small voice, 'The vortex.' Then he asked, 'What did the Control Tower say just before the ship's thrusters were started?' 'Gravity net on full.' And what were the words for where the ship went? 'Coordinates of the planetary destination.' On and on the questions went, with the doctor growing more and more excited. Finally he put his questionnaire down and asked me if I would like to play a game. A mind game. He would attach me to a little portable amplifier he carried and show me things I couldn't see with my eyes. I let him put the headset on my temples, then he hit the switch, and my whole world exploded."

She grimaced in shared pain as Wander continued, "I remember screaming, but not much else. It seemed as though it took him hours to turn it off and get the headset off my head."

"Hours and hours," Consuela agreed.

"I must have fainted, because the next thing I knew, I was in a hospital bed, and my mother was leaning over me, stroking my forehead and crying. When I opened my eyes and felt the world spinning, she made it a lot worse by screaming to the doctor, who was still with me, that he had destroyed my brain. Finally he quieted her and leaned over me and said that he was very sorry, that somehow the amplifier had been turned up too high, it was a terrible mistake, but there should be no permanent damage. After an hour or so things were a lot better, and my mother calmed down, and she let me speak with the doctor alone. He told me that there was a good chance that I was a Talent, and he would need to give me more tests. There was a problem, though, and because he had hurt me he wanted to tell me about it.

"He said that all children lost some of their Talent as

they passed through puberty, did I know that word? More than nine-tenths of all children who tested positive at earlier ages lost it completely. And the more sensitive the child, the greater the likelihood that the loss would be total. So the Hegemony did not do anything except register sensitive children. Doctors like him were working on the problem night and day, but they had not discovered either the reason or a cure. I listened to what he said and decided I didn't mind. Well, I did, but not too much. I liked watching the ships take off, but other than that, Talent had done nothing but make my life miserable. I had no friends. Most people, including my family, thought I was crazy. No, I decided I wouldn't mind it all that much if my Talent disappeared."

"But it didn't," she said quietly.

"No," he agreed. "On my fifteenth birthday I was taken to a big hall and tested again. There were a *lot* of people there. Most of the children came with their families, and almost all the families were rich. They were different from me. They wore nice clothes and they spoke with different tones. They looked down their noses at me. So did a lot of the teachers. So I did what I did best. I retreated inside and tried to disappear."

"I know the feeling," Consuela said, her eyes calling out their sympathy.

"I learned a lot that day. It's amazing what you can hear and learn when people think you're of no account."

"They ignore you and forget that you're even there," Consuela agreed.

"I learned that children could receive special training as they passed through puberty that helped them hold on to their sensitivity," Wander continued. "I learned that it was only privately available, and that it was *extremely* expensive. I learned that the government kept it that way, because they preferred to see sensitivity be given to people whose station taught them how to use it responsibly. Those were the exact words I heard: To use their sensitivity in a responsible manner for the good of the Hegemony."

"The field," Consuela said. "You sat out there and watched the ships. That was your training."

"Maybe." Wander leaned forward, his voice intense. "I learned something else. Something other than the fact that most of the highborn people despised me, and felt I had no business being there. Something other than the fact that entry into scout training was extremely competitive. I learned that these rich kids, with all their special training, were not all that sensitive. I could run rings around them."

"So you hid your abilities," Consuela said, giving her head the barest of nods. "Smart."

"Yes," he agreed, drinking her in. "But here I learned that a Talent is someone who has what they call hypersensitivity, which means the ability to 'hear' with only a small amount of amplification. This is the first sign that the person can be trained to guide a starship through null-space. A couple of times I read about people who can 'hear' without any amplification at all. They're talked about like they were freaks."

"Have you talked to Senior Pilot Grimson?"

"I've been afraid to," he replied quietly. "When I arrived here, I discovered that Talents only come through here once every couple of years, so rare that a lot of people aren't even sure what they are. Then I started hearing strange rumors. Frightening ones. Of scouts who came here and then partway through training just disappeared. Taken for experimentation. Never heard from again. I worried that maybe these were people like me, and the scientists used them to see if they could breed for Talent." Slowly Wander shook his head. "I don't want to let anything come between me and space."

Consuela released his hand and began softly stroking his wrist. Her touch sent electric tingles through his body. "So Wander has remained the lonely little boy."

"I've had a lot of experience," he said. "Can I ask you a question?"

"Anything," she replied. "Anything at all."

"Have you ever been tested?"

"Never."

"Then how did you wind up here?"

"I have some secrets of my own, and when I'm feeling better I want to tell you about them." She hesitated, then added, "If I'm still here."

"They won't be letting you go, that's for certain," Wander assured her. "I need to ask you something else. When we were out there on the field, did you hear the countdown?"

"Yes."

He could scarcely keep his voice from betraying his excitement. "When the fifteen-second mark was hit, did you notice anything?"

"It felt," she groped for words, "like time was being stretched."

Wander felt the band of pressure tighten across his chest. "Where did the ship go?"

She searched her returning memory, then said in confusion, "Antari. I know where it is, but I've never heard of it before. How is that possible?"

His voice shaky, he said, "You don't know how long I've dreamed of this."

She looked at him a long moment, and for some reason her eyes brimmed with sorrow. "Oh, Wander."

"Someone to talk to," he went on. "Someone who understands."

"If only," she bit her lip, then sighed the words, "if only I could stay."

He laughed with relief. "They'd never let a Talent go. Not if you painted yourself green and ran screaming down the halls at midnight."

"Not much chance of that," she said and to his great joy smiled a second time. "Thank you for sharing your story with me."

"I haven't ever told anyone about it before," he confessed.

"I know," she said. "Come here."

He leaned forward. "What?"

"Closer," she said, raising her face to meet his, guiding him down with one cool hand on his neck, and kissing him with lips that were soft and warm and tasted just as he thought they should.

–Nine–

"Up and at 'em, Ensign," barked a voice near his head. "Captain Arnol wants you."

Rick opened bleary eyes and focused on a barrel-shaped man blocking the doorway. "What?"

"Down with mind-lag? Tough. On this ship, what the captain wants, the captain gets. And right now he wants you. Flight deck. On the bounce."

Rick rolled out of his bunk, only to find that his legs would barely support him. A hand twice the size of his own gripped his upper arm.

"Still suffering, are you? Don't worry, I've seen worse, and they always get better. Nobody ever dies from mind-lag. They just wish they could."

Rick struggled to focus on the man who held him upright. He was dressed in a flashy uniform, the dark green shoulders piped with gold braid and the sleeves bearing numerous gold slash marks. Something triggered in the recesses of his foggy brain, and he asked, "Chief Petty Officer?"

The barrel-chested man grinned. "Name is Tucker. I heard they boarded you on a stretcher. Don't worry about it. First time in null-space hits a lot of people hard. You're an outworlder, I hear. Where do you call home, son?"

"Baltimore," Rick mumbled.

The grin broadened. "Now that must have been a journey from the back of beyond. I've been shipping more than twenty Standard years, and I've never come across that name before." Experienced eyes checked his appearance. "Well, your uniform doesn't appear too much the worse for wear, seeing as how you've slept in it almost across the Hegemony. Come along then, and easy does it. Just put your weight on me until your legs get to working."

Uniform. Rick cast a glance down at his form and would have lost his footing save for Petty Officer Tucker's strong grip. He was dressed head to toe in palest gray, cut like the petty officer's, except without the slash marks. The material caught the light and shimmered in faint rainbow hues. His trousers were tucked into boots of the same material. Two rows of small gold buttons paraded up the front of his shirt, and his cuffs were trimmed with a single thin line of gold braid. He craned and saw that each of his shoulders bore a tiny gold pip.

A *uniform*.

The information was there in his mind. How, he could not explain. Yet still he knew. Ship's officers wore uniforms of gray—the higher the rank, the darker the uniform. Ensigns stood upon the bottom rung. Noncoms and flight technicians wore green—chief petty officers and senior scientists were top of the list. Scouts wore pale blue robes, communicators royal blue, pilots midnight blue.

But what was a pilot?

While Rick was still busy examining himself, Tucker guided him into the chute. It was only when his weight dropped away that he glanced up and gasped.

The petty officer was vastly pleased with the reaction.

"Now that's what I like to see. A youngster who's not above showing a little pride in a ship of the line. Grand, isn't she?"

Dumbly, Rick nodded. Grand indeed she was. The chute tracked itself up one wall, while below extended a vast surface of bustling activity. Great sparkling machinery and strange-looking equipment were monitored by numerous personnel in uniforms of pearl white. The words popped unbidden into his mind: specialist technicians assigned off-world duty.

"Ah, coming around, now, are you? Good." Nothing escaped the chief petty officer's perception. "So tell me, Ensign, what is it you're looking at?"

"Outer cargo hold," Rick said, bemused. He could not say how he knew, but know he did. "Used for oversized freight and consignments requiring preparation while in shipment."

Tucker grunted his approval. "What's that contraption over in the corner, then?"

The enormous multi-sided globe was all polarized windows and energy reflectors, with various arms and drills and scoops sprouting at odd points. It shone like a polished bronze sphere. Rick said in confused wonderment, "A three-man mining pod, designed for solar-proximity worlds."

"And that tin can there at your feet?"

Rick looked down, saw a massive steel-gray canister being inspected by a score of technicians, and felt the information click into his consciousness. "A retrievable drone for surface studies under extremely adverse conditions such as corrosive atmosphere, ultra-high atmospheric pressures, or hostile inhabitants."

"You'll do," the chief petty officer decided. "Straighten up now, we're on final approach."

The chute continued through several upper levels before emerging into the flight deck's antechamber. Rick stepped out after his guardian, felt gravity resurge, and followed him through doors marked with strange signings that he somehow knew read "Flight and Comm Deck. Authorized Personnel Only." He stepped through the portal and gasped a second time.

"Here's your fresh meat, Captain Arnol," the petty officer announced.

"Two arms, two legs, a head, all limbs still intact," a hatchet-faced man said, swiveling his chair around. "You were gentle on the lad, Tuck."

"There's time for paring him down if the need arises," the petty officer replied. "Right now the boy's barely got the strength to hold himself upright."

Rick felt an elbow nudge him, and he dragged his eyes away from the vista spread out before him. Somehow he knew what was expected. "Ensign Richard reporting for duty, sir."

"Richard, Richard. Don't believe I've come across that one before. What sort of label is that, Ensign?"

"It, ah, belonged to a famous king, Captain. He was known as the Lionhearted."

"Your own kings, is it? Ah yes, now I recall. You're an outworlder. Well, we don't hold a shipmate's origins against him, not on this ship. What counts is performance."

Captain Arnol was a taut man, his actions measured and swift. He plucked a form from the pouch attached to one arm of his chair. "Your record is impressive, Ensign, as far as it goes. But book learning and athletic skills interest me only if they can be transferred to ship duty. That's why the Hegemony requires ensigns to serve aboard ship before their tour at the academy. You with me?"

"Yes, Captain."

"Your uniform says ensign, but in reality you are junior

to every bosun's mate on this ship. The reason is simple. They are experienced spacers, and you are a raw recruit. Nothing will earn you a downcheck faster in their eyes or mine than putting on airs you don't deserve."

The captain tossed the sheet aside. "Over the next ten weeks, you'll be serving on every level of this ship. There is no duty that you can refuse, nothing that is beneath your level. If the chief petty officer orders you to scrub the main cargo deck with a toothbrush, I expect you to carry out your orders with a smile. You follow?"

"Yes, Captain." Rick could not help it. His eyes tracked upward as though drawn on their own will. He was looking at it and still could not believe what he saw.

When the silence dragged on, he glanced back to find the captain smiling thinly. "Never been on a flight deck before, have you, Ensign?"

"No, Captain," he replied weakly. "First time."

"Ever spaced before?"

"No, Captain," he said and let his eyes coast back up.

"You mean the trip from your homeworld was your first time outbound?"

A lean little man in the seat next to the captain gave a chuckle. Rick recognized the position as belonging to the helmsman. "Raw isn't the word for this one, Skipper."

"Quiet," Captain Arnol said mildly. "I suppose it wouldn't hurt for you to join us for the landing, Ensign. Understand, though, you'll make up all duties the chief petty officer may have for you before going ashore."

"Look at the poor guy," the helmsman said. "He's all eyes and mouth."

"Quiet, I said. All right, son. Take a seat, no, not that one, that's the pilot's chair. Remember that. This position of every flight deck is reserved for the pilot, whether or not the ship carries one. Which we don't, since we're on planetary duty inside Hegemony boundaries."

"And good riddance," muttered the other officer. The captain let it pass without comment.

Rick let himself be steered into an empty seat by the inside wall. He nodded when ordered to report to Chief Petty Officer Tucker after they touched down, yet he scarcely gave it conscious thought. All he could see, all he could take in, was the vista in front of him.

The flight deck was split into two segments. The lower half was one unbroken mass of instrumentation and switches and flickering lights and complex read-out systems. Each chair spun on its own free axis and had a series of banked instruments that slid up alongside each arm or glided on transparent wings up and over the chair's head. Rick found himself aware that each seat was called a station, and that each station had a name—Captain, Watch Commander, Communications Specialist, Pilot, Helmsman, Weapons, Assistant Watch Officer, Power Technician, and so on around the room.

But the growing sense of unbidden knowledge could not take away from what stretched out above him.

The other half of the chamber was a solid sheet of unbroken horizon. Rick knew that in truth it was a great series of interconnected screens joined to ultra-precise cameras set in the ship's nose. But this did not affect his awe for a second.

The ship was inbound for a planet that was already so close the blackness of space was limited to an encircling border. To his left, a small orbiting moon was spinning up and away behind them. The sun was just cresting the planet's upper horizon, crowning the hazy atmosphere with a broad sweep of flame. Directly before him, a brilliant blue sky was flecked with swatches of white cloud.

"Might as well switch on his seat," the captain instructed. "Give him the full effect."

"Aye, aye, Captain."

For a third time, shock punched the breath from his body. Rick felt as well as saw a golden ribbon race out from the ship, connecting it to a pulsating beacon located down below the clouds. It was the ITN, he knew without knowing how—the interplanetary transport network. In shipboard slang, the ITN was called a lightway. Ships transversing the inner Hegemony locked into the appropriate target-route and rode on semi-automatic the entire way.

Yet his awareness of these facts was buffeted by the other effect which was now coursing through his mind and body. The seat was now connected to him, and through this coupling came a sensation unlike anything he had ever known.

Power.

–TEN–

The next morning found Consuela standing on the highest of the seven balconies that looked out over the vast spaceport arena. She felt she could spend days watching the scene spread out before her. Behind her, the field itself was visible through thick shielded windows, but for the moment she was content to ignore the ships' comings and goings. There was simply too much else to take in.

Directly in front of her rose an unbroken wall of polarized glass eight stories high and two hundred yards wide. Through it she watched hovercraft descend, deposit passengers and personnel, and silently depart. Beyond the unloading bay stretched a vast surface filled with personal vehicles the likes of which she had never even imagined. Part wheelless car and part glider, their stubby wings retracted as the carriers slowed and settled to earth.

Seven stories below her stretched the bustling port's colorful panorama. Wander had been correct—the floor's directional lights did look like a multicolored spider web. Consuela watched as people entered, stated their business to the information column, and then haughtily ignored the pulsating ribbons of light. From her lofty position she could stare with abandon at their obvious wealth and station. Highborn passengers wore beautiful clothes and bored expressions, as though determined not to be impressed by anything they saw. Every few moments the entire structure hummed with the power of departing spaceships. Consuela was the only person who paid the slightest notice.

"Ah, there you are."

Consuela turned to confront a slender boy who eyed her with disdain. The boy went on, "Watching the animals go through their paces, are we?"

"I've never seen anything like this," she replied honestly.

The boy's air of superiority strengthened. "Yes, we hear all sorts of ghastly tales about primitive outworld societies. How did you survive?"

"I kept my spear sharpened at all times," Consuela replied calmly. Maybe it wasn't so different here after all.

An angry glint appeared at the notice that she gave as well as she got. "Pilot Grimson has chosen me to be his errand boy. He wishes to see you in the Tower."

"Where—"

The boy raised one haughty eyebrow. "Don't tell me an exceptional sensitive like yourself doesn't even know where the Tower is. Tsk, tsk. How shameful."

"I just arrived yesterday," she replied, her cheeks burning.

"Yes, so I heard." He turned around and sauntered off, tossing a parting remark over his shoulder. "I suggest you just reach out with all these powers of yours and find it for yourself."

She was still hot when she found the pilot waiting impatiently at the Tower entrance. "What took you so long?"

"A little snit of a scout who couldn't be bothered to show me where to go," she replied angrily.

"Ah," Pilot Grimson said, nodding his understanding. "Only to be expected."

"Maybe to you."

"Put yourself in his position," he said, for some reason showing her patience. "Child of a good family, given every opportunity to develop what sensitivity he has, only to arrive and discover that an outworlder, who is not even required to go through the horrors of culling, shows a level of Talent that he did not even imagine existed."

"It still doesn't excuse his bad manners," Consuela retorted.

"No, in a perfect world, it would not. But as we must deal with what we have, I suggest we move onward. How are you feeling?"

"Better. Still a little shaken, but better."

"Very well." He slipped back into his mantle of frosty control. "All scouts are required to stand training watches. For most it is a period of watching and learning and trying to hone their abilities through mind games. Scout Wander has shown a remarkable level of skill, however, and today will begin actual Tower Watch. As you have shown Talent potential, I want you to stand to his schedule."

"Fine with me," Consuela said, and could not suppress her grin of pleasure.

Grimson's eyes narrowed. "I also suggest you learn from Wander the correct manner in which to deport yourself with your superiors."

Still rankled by the scout's snipes, Consuela found that the pilot's lofty attitude struck a spark to dry tinder. "Wander is afraid of you."

He had clearly not expected that. "And you are not?"

"Wander lives for space. It's all he's ever wanted to do."

Consuela forced herself to meet the pilot's probing gaze. "He's terrified that a downcheck from you would hold him back."

"Remarkable how close you have become in such a short period," Grimson murmured.

Consuela felt her face go red, but stood her ground. "Maybe what he really needs from you is a compliment and a kind word."

The pilot studied her thoughtfully. "A scout who on her third day presumes herself ready to advise a pilot. . . Let us hope your Talent is sufficient to excuse such behavior. Come along."

She followed him through the great bronze portal. Immediately her mind was beset with a hundred buzzing voices. She entered a circular room perhaps fifty paces across, where several dozen people staffed complex consoles rising in curved rows. The globe's entire upper surface was transparent, granting an uninterrupted view of the fields and the ships and the spaceport roof.

His headset already in place, Wander stood at nervous attention on the right-hand dais, a broad elevated platform that looked down and out over the Tower activities. A young woman in robes of royal blue sat beside him, operating a half-moon console of bewildering complexity. Two additional chairs with smaller consoles stood behind her, unmanned.

Pilot Grimson started for the side stairs, but was immediately halted by a graying man with a dark brown uniform and a very irritated manner. "Just a moment, if you please, Pilot."

"Can it wait?" Grimson asked testily.

"No, it cannot." The man stepped directly in front of him. "As watch commandant, I formally protest this action."

"Your protest is noted. Now if you will please step aside—"

"I insist that my protest and your response be formally logged," the man persisted.

Grimson gave an exasperated sigh. "Very well, Commandant. Lead on." To Consuela he said, "Wait here, Scout."

As the pilot moved off, Consuela tried to give Wander a reassuring smile, but the noise in her head was as persistent as a dentist's drill.

The watch commandant stepped to a solitary console set on the central dais, separated by a valley of stairs from Wander's platform. He touched a switch and said, "Tower Log official entry. Watch Commandant Loklin speaking. I wish to officially protest granting the Scout Wander full watch status. Having only completed two months of the training program, the scout is not qualified for such action, which I believe places the activity of the entire port in serious jeopardy."

Consuela saw Wander's jaw drop open. She wanted to rush to him and share in the moment even though she was not sure exactly what it meant, but she was held captive by the infernal buzzing voices.

Meeting the commandant's angry gaze, Grimson replied, "Senior Pilot Grimson responding. I hereby officially override the commandant's objection and assign the Scout Wander to full watch."

The commandant viciously punched the switch and snapped, "You are making a grave error, Pilot."

"And you are in for a very big surprise," the pilot responded.

"I hope so," the commandant said, glaring at Wander. "For all our sakes, I very much hope so."

Grimson came back around the curving walk, and as he

drew close he noticed Consuela's distress. "What is the matter?"

"Voices," she said. "They won't stop."

A blaze of triumph lit the pilot's features. "Voices?"

"In my head," she replied, struggling not to wince. "It *hurts*."

"Follow me." He turned and walked up the side stairs to where Wander stood by the platform's polished railing. He extracted a small apparatus from his belt pouch, picked up a headset, and attached it just above the temple pad. He fitted it to Consuela's forehead, then stepped back. "How is that?"

"A little better," she said, so relieved that the painful buzzing was diminishing she even smiled at the frosty old man.

"But still there?"

"Yes."

For some reason, her response increased the pilot's triumph. He took her hand, guided it up to the little box, said, "There is a dial recessed into the surface. Feel the edge? Good. Now turn the dial until the sound disappears."

Consuela spun the little dial, and as the buzzing voices faded into silence, she let out a grateful sigh. "They're gone."

"Excellent." Pilot Grimson turned to Wander. "This is the one you have altered?"

"Yes, Pilot."

"Take it off."

Still bemused, Wander did as he was ordered. Shaking his head, the pilot inspected the headset. Then he set it down, picked up a different set, extracted a second apparatus from his pouch, and fitted it on. He handed it over and said, "Try this. Use the dial as I instructed."

To Consuela's surprise, Wander gave a blissful smile. "Amazing."

"You heard them too?" she asked him.

"All the time," he replied. "Until now."

"How could you stand it?"

"It was hard. Very hard."

"Enough," the pilot ordered. He pointed to the communication console and said to Wander, "You must adjust the amplification so that all directed signals are clearly audible. I assume this is what you have been doing all along?"

"Yes, Pilot."

"Very well." He raised his voice so that it carried through the Tower. "Scout Wander, you are now assigned full watch duty."

From his central station, the commandant released an angry snort. Grimson turned so that he watched the back of the commandant's head as he continued, "You have for the past two weeks been acting under the direct guidance of a senior communicator who has done nothing but monitor your activities."

Slowly the commandant swiveled his chair about and looked at Wander in surprise. Grimson went on, "You have performed faultlessly. I expect you to continue doing so. The safety of this port is now in your hands."

"Yes, Pilot," Wander managed. His look of ecstasy was almost painful to Consuela.

The pilot nodded and walked back down the side stairs. At the portal he turned and addressed the Tower as a whole, "For the sake of harmony within the scout squadron, I ask you all to say nothing of this development."

The Tower remained frozen, all attention focused on Wander, until a voice called, "Incoming."

The Tower sprang back to life. All but the watch commandant, who kept his gaze fastened on the scout.

Wander turned and nervously said, "I relieve you, Communicator."

"Eleven Hegemony ships," the communicator droned, "all in proper ascendance-descendance, channels two, seven, four. Three starships approaching transcendence, note the channels."

"Noted," Wander said, his eyes luminous.

The woman stood. "There are fourteen listed departures for the next hour. All on schedule, plus-or-minus the acceptable limits."

"Noted," Wander repeated.

"Very well." She keyed the console and stated, "Specialist Communicator Evana logging out."

"Scout Wander logging on," he said, his voice strengthening.

The auburn-haired woman inspected Consuela, gave them both a minuscule nod, and said, "Good luck."

His hands already busy on the controls, Wander motioned Consuela into the seat to the right and behind his own. She sat and watched as he reached over her console, pointed to the central pulsing dial, and said, "Amplifier. Raise it to where you can comfortably hear me and the incoming messages." Hastily he hit three keys, said, "I have locked your channel onto mine. Just sit and watch. It will all begin to make sense in time."

Commandant Loklin gave her a hostile inspection, then dismissed them with a shake of his head and swung back around. Consuela felt other gazes on them from about the room but was determined not to respond. Very slowly she swung the amplifier dial until voices became audible in her head. But this time they were single voices, and held to a comfortable level.

And Wander's was one of them.

"Starship Excelsior, this is Hegemony Port. You are

scheduled for transition in six minutes and counting."

"Port, this is Excelsior," came the droning reply. "Six-minute mark noted."

Wander thumbed a switch on his chair's arm and said more quietly, "Can you hear me?"

"Yes."

"There's no need to talk out loud. Just move your lips. It helps shape the words. I know this is all very confusing, but there is no other way to learn."

She found herself thrilling to the intimacy of this contact. "Congratulations."

He angled his chair her way just long enough to show his grateful smile. "This is a dream come true."

"I know."

"Just a minute." He ran through a series of switches, and with each she heard a different voice. Wander did not speak until keying the final switch, when he droned, "Watch notes quarter-hour sweep, all in order and on schedule."

He then keyed his chair and said, "When you see me hit this switch, we can talk. Otherwise you need to just watch and listen."

"I understand."

"Most of watch is oversight. Sensitives are the only ones capable of interstellar communication, unless a drone is sent through null-space carrying something too confidential for the normal relay. Normal communication bands are held to the speed of light. You've probably heard this before."

"None of it," she confessed.

"Don't worry, it'll come soon. Sensitives are assigned watch duty to check a ship's transition and confirm that everything is in order." He paused as a vast beehive of burnished metal lowered itself onto a brilliant platform of fire.

"Hegemony vessel. They travel along lightways, or ITN target-routes. Lightways traverse Hegemony planetary systems and punch through n-space on short patterns in constant use. For all other routes, a pilot is responsible for ship's transition."

Things became increasingly busy then, and Wander had scarce moments to speak with her. She did not mind. Consuela was happy to sit and watch the harried bustling take on a tight sense of order. Wander monitored all incoming and outgoing vessels, communicated with all ports either receiving or dispensing ships. Tracking codes were accepted by other staff, who barked back landing and takeoff instructions, which were passed on by Wander. The watch commandant said little, but his eyes missed nothing. Each time he glanced her way, Consuela felt his searing frustration scorch her where she sat.

In a quiet moment, she asked, "Why do they look at us like that?"

Wander did not need to ask what she meant. "Nobody much likes a pilot."

"But why?"

"Passengers call us the ship magicians. When you go out in public in your robes, you'll be addressed as wizard. People say we speak with ghosts and control dark forces. The staff have other names for us. Freakos, pointy heads, amp junkies—those you'll hear a lot."

"That's a lot of nonsense."

"Get used to it," he replied. "There's nothing else you can do. I hear it's the same shipboard. Captains don't like sharing power and having to rely on us for the transitions. I heard one say the Hegemony would be better off finding another way to chart their vessels, one that fits to the proper scheme of things."

In the far lower corner, opposite the main tower entrance, a second set of doors opened into the staff compound. Every time a flight landed, a formal transfer was made to the ground crew who occupied the bottom two rows of consoles. They assigned the ship to a free terminal, directed refueling and mechanics and cleanup and staffing and the myriad of tasks that prepared the ship for its next departure. An officer entered the lower door after each landing, saluted the crewperson staffing the first console, and handed over the ship's documents. They were distributed, inspected, stamped, coded, and returned.

Beyond the transparent globe, four thruster shields were spaced equidistant about the central field. Peripheral fields were given over to ships awaiting transition, freighters being loaded for night departure slots, ships undergoing major repairs, storage sheds, private vessels in longer-term storage, and military craft. Every few minutes an internal Hegemony vessel would lift off or arrive in smoothly humming precision.

Once every quarter hour a brilliant gravity net would peel open in an awesome display of barely controlled power, releasing a ship into the swirling nothingness of null-space. Timed in similar cadence, a vortex would suddenly appear above an empty thruster shield, and suddenly a ship would appear in a white-gold flash of light. Consuela noticed how Wander would key them out of direct contact with the ship just before the fifteen-second count was coded. She understood him perfectly. He had other duties that would not give him the interval necessary to recover from having time stretched.

After two hours of almost constant activity, Wander's robe was growing damp spots under his arms and at the small of his back. His voice was steady but hoarse. Several times he paused long enough to wipe the perspiration away from his eyes.

A few minutes later the main portal opened to admit a heavy-set woman with a head of tightly clenched curls. As she treaded up the stairs to the communicator's platform, she did not bother to cover her astonishment. "You are standing watch?"

"Yes, Communicator," Wander replied.

"A scout handling full watch?" Her cheeks sprouted two red spots. "Who authorized this?"

"Senior Pilot Grimson," Commandant Loklin said dryly, swiveling his chair around to face Wander. "You may tell the pilot that he was correct. I have indeed been surprised."

"Thank you, Commandant," Wander said, rising to his feet.

The woman demanded, "How long have you been in training, Scout?"

"Two months." Wander pointed to the flickering console. "Fifteen Hegemony vessels, all coded on channels seven and nine. Four—"

"Get off my platform," she snapped. "Now."

Wander bowed his head in weary acceptance. He coded the message board and stated quietly, "Scout Wander logging out."

"Communicator Zenna logging in," she stated in fury, and kept her hand on the key as she continued, "What utter mess have you left me with?"

Wander motioned with his head for Consuela to follow him down. As they approached the portal, Commandant Loklin called out, "Scout Wander."

Wander straightened. "Yes, Commandant."

"You may tell the senior pilot," the commandant replied, "that you are welcome to stand duty on my watch at any time."

It took Wander a moment before he could reply. "Thank you, Commandant."

Consuela turned to toss a gloat back toward the outraged communicator, when she caught sight of something out of the corner of her eye. She seized Wander's arm. "Wait a second."

"What's the matter?" He followed her eyes and said, "It's just another ensign logging in his ship."

"No, it's not," she cried. "That's *Rick*!"

–Eleven–

They did not like each other. That much was clear even before introductions were made.

No question about it, Rick looked incredibly dashing in his uniform. As the three of them walked the crew's passage back to his gate, every female crew member who passed granted him frankly assessing glances. Consuela would have enjoyed the questioning attention that consequently landed upon her, except for Wander. After the excitement she had shown over seeing Rick, Wander had retreated into his silent shell and had not emerged.

The passage forked, one way leading through customs and out into the port proper, the other back toward the eastport terminal gates. Wander stopped and announced, "I think I should report back to Pilot Grimson."

Consuela found herself reluctant to let him go. "Can't you leave it for just a little while?"

"I can see you want to speak with your homeworld friend," he said quietly, refusing even to look in Rick's direction.

"Yeah, look, I don't have much time," Rick agreed. "My ship's scheduled to lift off, soon as we onload a shipment."

Consuela found herself hurting from the look of sorrow in Wander's eyes. "He's just a friend," she said softly.

"Of course," Wander replied. He gave them a stiff nod and walked down the outgoing passage.

Consuela stayed where she was, watching his retreating back, until Rick pressed, "I've got to be getting back. They keep me on a short leash."

"Okay," she said and walked on, trying to collect herself. "What are you *doing* here?"

"What do you think?" Rick flashed his famous grin. "I came to rescue you."

She felt herself growing hot. "I can take care of myself."

"Sure, sure." Under the gaze of three attractive crew women, Rick's walk took on a swagger. "Anyway, do you want to hear what happened or not?"

"Tell me."

As she listened to his story, Consuela found herself thinking more of Wander than of the world she had left behind. Rick finished with, "The craziest thing is how I know all this stuff. Everything about the ship, you name it, I know it. Has that happened to you too?"

"No. But I have," she hesitated, then settled on, "some new abilities."

"Yeah, you're wearing a scout's robes. That means you're a sensitive, right?"

"Yes." He had looked so sad. Consuela gazed up at Rick, comparing his easy strength and unshakable confidence with Wander's quiet reserve. No, there wasn't any question whom she preferred.

"See what I mean? There's no way I could know anything like that." He pointed down a branch passage. "This is my gate."

Consuela tried to push her heart's concerns aside. "So do you want to go back home?"

"Yeah, sure. I mean, I've got to, right?" Then he turned and looked down the branch passage. "Do you think all this is real?"

"I don't know what to think."

"Me neither. Sure seems—"

"Ensign, is your captain on board?"

Consuela started at the sound of the voice echoing down the passageway and turned to see Grimson and Wander rapidly approaching. She watched Rick come stiffly to full alert and reply, "Should be. We're scheduled for lift-off soon."

"Find him, please. Tell him that Senior Pilot Grimson urgently needs to speak with him."

"Yes, Pilot."

"No, better still, we will follow you on board. This matter cannot wait." Brusquely the pilot motioned him forward. "Lead on, Ensign. Come along, you two."

Consuela fell into step alongside Wander. As the other two pulled ahead, she whispered, "What's going on?"

Wander shook his head. "He was looking for me. I've never seen him run—"

"Silence," Grimson rapped out.

The passage jinked and opened into a broad loading platform. Landing crew entered through the cargo passage. They manipulated hand controls to guide wheelless handcarts up the ramp and through the broad ship's portal. Two of the ship's crew inspected documents, checked each item off their noteboards, and assigned a hold number before permitting passage. When Grimson came into view, both crewmen snapped to startled attention.

"Ensign Richard with visitors for the captain," Rick announced, and the change in his voice caused Consuela to look at him anew.

The senior crewman raised his noteboard. "Names?"

"Senior Pilot Grimson and two scouts," the pilot snapped.

"I'll call him downside," the crewman said.

"You'll do no such thing. The matter is most urgent. I demand immediate entry."

Clearly the crewman had no interest in a confrontation with an irate pilot. "He's in the top outer hold with the supercargo."

"Notify him of our arrival. Lead on, Ensign. Hurry, man, hurry." Grimson motioned for Consuela and Wander to follow.

Consuela caught fleeting glimpses of vast holds, incredibly strange machinery, bustling technicians. As she rode the chute alongside Wander, she was gratified to see that the excitement of being in a ship had erased his earlier sorrow.

She took the moment of relative privacy to whisper, "Everything's all right, Wander. Really."

Wander tore his gaze from the vista beneath them. His face took on somber lines as he said, "The ensign is very handsome."

"Very," Consuela agreed.

"And he is from your homeworld. You must have a lot in common."

"Some. But we are still just friends."

"Why are you telling me this?"

She tried hard to open her gaze. "It's important to me that you understand, Wander. Rick is not a threat to us."

"To us?" he repeated softly.

"That's right," she said. "Us."

He started to speak, then glanced up. "They're disembarking."

Consuela turned away, stepped out, adjusted to the gravity change, and followed the pilot and Rick across the deck toward a pair of stout hold doors. But before they could push through, a hatchet-faced man came out, followed by a portly man carrying a bundle of forms. The sharp-edged officer wore a uniform of darkest gray dressed with numerous gold insignias. "Senior Pilot Grimson?"

"Captain Arnol." The pilot gave a little bow. "Thank you for seeing me."

The captain maintained his cold rigidity. "I understand the matter is so urgent you could not obey proper procedures."

"That is correct. I would ask a favor."

That startled him. "A pilot asks a favor of a Hegemony freighter captain?"

"I understand that you are outbound and due to return here again in nine days' time."

"All that is a matter of record."

"I would ask that you take these two scouts with you on a training run."

Wander gasped aloud. Captain Arnol eyed him, then turned his attention back to the pilot. "This is most unusual."

"Indeed. So are the circumstances." Grimson held himself stiffly erect. "I would consider myself in your debt, Captain."

The captain studied him. "I have heard that Senior Pilot Grimson is a man of his word."

"You need but name your request, Captain."

"You are perhaps aware," Arnol replied slowly, "that I am up for consideration as captain of a new outbound passenger vessel."

"I was not," Grimson replied. "But I shall make it my business to become fully involved in the matter."

The captain unbent enough to nod once, then turned his

attention to the two scouts. "How long have they been in training?"

"Scout Wander for just over two months. Scout Consuela for less than one week."

"A *week*?" The captain's ire mounted. "You are saddling me with a novice?"

Pilot Grimson hesitated, then said quietly, "They are both Talents."

Rick mirrored the captain's astonishment. "You're sure?"

"Absolutely certain."

"Two Talents based at this port?"

"Two Talents in the same scout squadron," Grimson replied. "And I have just received word that a diplomat is arriving this very afternoon."

"Ah. I understand your dilemma." Arnol hesitated, then said, "I must warn you, Pilot, that our destinations are Solarus and Avanti."

The pilot was clearly rocked by the news. "I wondered why the destinations were not stated on your manifest."

"As you can see, we have reasons for secrecy."

Grimson thought his way through a deep breath. "I have no choice. Yours is the only vessel scheduled for a swift return that departs before the diplomat's arrival."

"Very well." Captain Arnol turned to Rick and ordered, "Take them to Chief Petty Officer Tucker. Have him assign berths. Then get below and prepare for lift-off."

"Aye, aye, sir."

"You have earned a pilot's gratitude," Grimson said solemnly.

"No small matter. You must excuse me now, Pilot. We are approaching the final countdown, and I have a ship to run." Captain Arnol returned the pilot's bow, then said to Wander and Consuela, "Follow whoever gives you instructions. Stay in your berths until either I or the chief petty officer sends for you. A novice scout carries no authority on this ship. Step out of line, and you'll stand punishment detail like any other shipmate. Understand?"

"Yes, Captain," they chorused.

"I see they have landed in the correct pair of hands," Grimson said, then turned to the pair and ordered, "I have taken on a debt because of you. Repay me with correct shipboard service. I will give Captain Arnol's report my most careful scrutiny." He inspected them for a long moment, then walked to the down-chute and disappeared.

"All right," the captain barked. "Departure stations. On the bounce."

– TWELVE –

Consuela found the wait incredibly boring. Her cubbyhole had the same featureless quality of her room at port, only smaller. There was a limit to the amount of time she could nap, especially when she knew she was in a ship under power.

After what felt like days, the door opened to reveal Rick. He grinned and said, "The chief petty officer wants you on deck, Scout."

"Finally." She leapt from the seat, checked her hair in the mirror, and followed him into the passageway. "I never thought space could be so boring."

"Get used to it," he replied, stopping in front of Wander's door.

"What do you mean?"

"I'll let Petty Officer Tucker tell you." Rick made no move to open the portal. "Who is this guy, Consuela?"

"Wander is a friend. A good friend."

"Wander," he snickered. "What a name."

"He is the finest person I've ever met."

"That so?"

"Yes," she replied. "It is."

Rick did not show the jealousy she had half expected. Instead he seemed positively thrilled. "So you're falling for the guy."

"What if I am?"

"Hey, don't get me wrong. I think that's great."

"You sound relieved."

"Maybe so." Rick hesitated. "Last year I got burned by this girl back at school. I don't know, for some reason I was worried about you doing the same thing. But I haven't fallen for you, see, so everything's great. Really." He looked at her. "You don't think I'm a flake, do you?"

She started. It was exactly what she had been thinking. "I think you are too handsome for your own good," she said slowly. "And I think life is too easy for you."

Anger flared in his eyes. "That shows how well you know me."

"There's no need to get mad. You asked me what I thought."

"Yeah, well, thanks for nothing." He punched the door pad and watched Wander scramble to his feet. "Show time, sport. The chief petty officer doesn't like to be kept waiting. And watch yourselves in there. Something's got him in a bad state."

As they walked down the gently curving passageway, Consuela bumped up against Wander, swiftly grasped his hand, squeezed and released it. She felt a warm spot blossom in her heart with the delight that sprang to his face.

Still miffed, Rick asked as he walked, "You really think it's wise to get involved when we don't know how long—"

"Stop that," Consuela snapped back. "Right now."

"Just asking," he said, pleased to find a weak point. "I mean, you can't tell—"

"I'm warning you," Consuela declared.

Wander looked at her. "Is this the secret you wanted to tell me about?"

"Yes," she replied.

Rick stared over his shoulder. "You're going to try and explain it to him?"

"Lead on, Ensign," Consuela replied. "This is between Wander and me."

Rick snorted his derision. He stopped in front of a portal, keyed the intercom, and said, "Ensign Richard reporting with the two scouts."

"Enter."

The door sighed back to reveal one of the largest men Consuela had ever seen. He glanced up from his cluttered work station. "Scouts Wander and Consuela, do I have that right?" From beneath bushy eyebrows he gave them a dour inspection. "You have neither of you worked flight duty before, is that not also true?"

"I have never been on a ship before," Wander replied.

He glowered at them. "We ask for Starfleet help," he groused. "Every outbound voyage. We hear nothing for years on end, and now this?"

Consuela followed Wander's lead and said nothing.

"I am Chief Petty Officer Tucker, Tuck to my friends, which you two are most certainly not. I won't make any secret of it, I don't have much time for sensitives, nor do my crew. You'll be well advised to stay in your berths except when you're standing watch. Ensign Richard here has offered to escort you to and from flight deck and to deliver your meals."

"But that's like being in prison," Consuela protested.

"Not at all," the petty officer replied with vast satisfaction. "Ship's company have no right to order sensitives about; I know that as well as the next man. You're welcome to go anywhere you want, any time you want. But don't come crawling to me if some mate decides to let you have it. I guarantee your protection only if you obey my rules." He settled massive forearms on his paperwork and leaned forward. "Stay in your quarters if you know what's good for you."

"But why would they want to hurt us?" Consuela demanded. "I've never even seen the inside of a ship before."

"More's the pity," Tucker barked. "Let's just say that your kind has let us down one time too many." He glowered at them a moment longer, then picked up a form and said, "Now then. Captain Arnol says he wants to have you train together. Save him the need of repeating things. You sensitives are limited to a four-hour shift each Standard day, so—"

"I'd like to volunteer for more duty," Wander said and swiftly passed a look Consuela's way.

"Me too," she piped in.

He dropped the duty roster. "What's that?"

"I would like to go for watch and watch," Wander said.

The barrel-chested man leaned back in his chair and gave Wander a hard look. "You're telling me that we've got us a pair of sensitives who are volunteering for four hours on, four off?" He glanced at Rick. "Have you ever heard of a sensitive volunteering for anything, Ensign?"

"Chief Petty Officer, I—"

"Never mind." He lumbered to his feet. "This is one for the captain. Come along, all of you."

The hostility that flanked them between decks was as searing as a blowtorch. Consuela felt eyes burning into her from every direction. Clearly the crew had been alerted to their presence, and those they passed slowed and stared with undisguised loathing. She struggled to follow Wander's example and ignore them all.

She gasped at the star-flecked vista that greeted her inside the control room, but Captain Arnol granted them little time for relishing the view. He received the chief petty officer's report, then turned his knife-edged features their way and demanded, "Well? What have you got to say for yourselves?"

"Nothing, Captain," Wander replied. "We just want to volunteer for extra duty."

"None of your kind ever volunteers for anything," he snapped. "I'd rather play nanny to a shipload of dowagers than spend one watch with most sensitives. Your Pilot Grimson is an exception, I'll grant you that. Did he put you up to this?"

"No, Captain."

"If this is somebody's idea of a prank, they'll be scrubbing the thruster tubes while we're still under power, and before this watch is over, I can promise you that." A snicker rose from the chamber's far corner, until the captain whirled about and lashed out, "Quiet." He then turned back and demanded, "Let's have the real reason, and right smart, mister. And mark my words, I won't stand for nonsense from you or anybody else."

"I've waited all my life for this moment," Wander said quietly.

The few heads still bent over instruments rose and joined the others staring their way.

"What's that?" Arnol said.

"Going to space is all I've ever dreamed of," Wander replied.

The captain's gaze narrowed as he searched Wander's face. "You're telling me you *want* to stand watch on a Hegemony freighter?"

"It's still space," Wander replied. "I want to learn."

The attention swung to bore into Consuela. "You have anything to add to that?"

"I wouldn't give most of the sensitives I've met the time of day," Consuela said.

"You don't say," the captain said slowly. "Chief Petty Officer, have you ever heard the like?"

"Never in all my born days, Skipper."

The captain backed two paces and settled into his chair. He pointed to his right, where a seat stood isolated behind a separate console, and said, "Observe, if you please. That is the pilot's chair. How long have I been skippering this freighter, Tucker?"

"Going on five and a half years, Captain."

"And how often have you seen that chair occupied?"

"Not the first minute, Skipper. Not the very first."

"Signals," he barked.

"Aye, aye, Captain."

"How many requests have you sent during this voyage for a sensitive to give us a hand?"

"Same as every voyage for the past seven months," the signals officer replied, his eyes never leaving the pair of them. "Once every Standard day."

"And what does our message book log in?"

"Same as what we've got outside our ports, Skipper," Signals replied. "A lot of nothing."

"So what happens," the captain went on, "but in the middle of a stopover, a senior pilot rushes up, asks me to do him the favor, the *favor*, of taking two Talents on board?"

There was a unison of indrawn breath around the room. From behind them, Chief Petty Officer Tucker asked, "So the scuttlebutt was true? They really are Talents?"

"So the senior pilot said. Mind you, he also told me that the boy here has had a grand total of two months' training, and the girl somewhat less. How much was it again, Scout?"

Consuela lifted her chin and replied, "Three days."

"Three days," Captain Arnol replied, nodding slowly. "So they are what you might call still novices. Still, the pilot sounded very definite about their abilities. Either of you ever spaced before?"

"No, Captain."

"So how did you know to volunteer for watch and watch?"

"I stood it in the Control Tower," Wander replied.

"Under a communicator's supervision, I take it."

"One watch I stood alone," Wander replied. "The one before we were brought on board."

The captain permitted himself a wintry smile. "Let us hope it was not so disastrous a watch that the pilot decided he had to be rid of you."

"The watch commandant said he would be happy to stand watch with Wander again," Consuela announced proudly.

"Did he now?" His eyes still on Consuela, Arnol said, "You ever heard of that one before, Tucker?"

"Definitely another for the books, Skipper."

The man next to the captain intoned, "Ten minutes to the first attack zone, Skipper."

"Thank you, Helmsman." He resumed his steely calm. "Chief Petty Officer, see if you and the ensign can swing a second chair behind the pilot's console."

"Aye, aye, Captain."

"Mind you disconnect the power supply," the captain said, swinging back around. "Hate to think what would happen if they had the mind amp and power chair on together."

"Maybe an improvement," suggested someone from the room's corner.

"Enough of that. Weapons team, power up."

"Weapons powered and full on, Captain."

"Signals?"

"Tracking and all clear."

"Thrusters?"

"One-third power, ready to redline on your command."

"Chief Petty Officer, the men are prepared?"

"All stations manned and ready, Skipper. They won't be boarding this vessel."

"Standard watches, Tucker. Can't have the men jumping at shadows the whole voyage."

"As you ordered, Skipper," the burly man replied, muscling a chair in behind the pilot's console. "But they'll be sleeping with one eye on the ready-light, believe you me."

"You two settle in," Captain Arnol ordered. "I have little experience in training sensitives—none at all, in fact. So for the time being I expect you to watch and listen and learn what you can. Know how to power a ship's amp?"

"I think so," Wander said hopefully, seating himself and running one excited hand over the console. "It looks a lot like the Tower controls."

"Five minutes, Skipper."

"Signals, ready to alert?"

"On your command, Captain."

"Everybody, stay awake."

Rick spoke up tentatively, "Request permission to stay, Captain."

"Any objections, Tucker?"

"None, sir."

"Then seat yourself and power on, son."

"Three minutes, Skipper."

Wander reached into his belt-pouch and brought out two headsets. "Grimson gave them to me back when he found me in the port passage," he whispered.

"It seems like years ago," Consuela said.

Wander nodded. "Turn the damping mechanism on full.

I'll start the amp on low, and power up slowly. Tell me when you're ready."

Consuela checked the dial, fitted her headset in place, and whispered, "Go ahead."

"Two minutes, Captain."

Slowly, very slowly Wander spun the console's central dial. "Feel anything?"

"Not yet. What's got everybody in a lather?"

"I don't know, but—" then he stopped. He had to. His attention was captured by the transformation in the vista overhead.

Consuela followed his gaze upward. Stretching out from the nose of the ship was a broad ribbon of golden light. She breathed, "What is *that?*"

"A lightway," Rick said quietly from behind them.

"Sixty seconds and counting," intoned the signals officer.

Consuela's heightened sensitivity gave her the feeling of stretching out beyond the flight deck, reaching out to every aspect of the ship. She reveled in the sensation of tracing her way through the myriad of passages, racing at the speed of thought from nose to powering thrusters.

"Fifteen seconds."

The ship was a chorus of signals and images, far too complex for her to take in, but wondrous in the sense of not just riding in a ship, but joining with it. Flying through space, intimately connected with the vessel and its power—

Then she leapt out of her seat with a shriek of disgust, and flung the headset across the room. Wander shouted and writhed and sent his headset spinning directly into the captain's back.

"Skipper, look!"

Consuela tore at her robes, flinging them about, then convulsively shook her head and body. She had the fleeting image of a million metal insects crawling all over her body, and she shrieked again.

Then it was gone.

She stood on shaky legs, her chest heaving. Wander raised himself from where he had been rubbing his body across the decks. He gasped, "Is it over?"

"Signals!" The captain's steel gray eyes gleamed with excitement. "Mark the spot!"

"On target, Skipper. To the decimal point."

"I was right!" Captain Arnol pounded the armrest, his gaze glued to the pair of scouts who struggled to gather themselves. "The shadowlanes are real!"

—Thirteen—

The atmosphere in the officers' mess was heavy with suspicion. Captain Arnol was held in too much esteem for the gathered officers to voice outright objections, yet they clearly resented having two young scouts granted entry, and resented eating in their company. Several of the more senior veterans shoved their plates aside untouched and fastened the pair with hostile glares.

Rick sat in the chair closest to the outer door and said not a word. His post was known as the Ensign's Corner, and he was placed there to do the bidding of whichever officer spoke in his direction. He stared as frankly as the others at Wander and Consuela. Their resolute calm had a disturbing effect on him. They seemed so *connected*. He could see from the briefest of glances that Consuela cast in Wander's direction that she was truly smitten with the guy. There was such love in her eyes, such admiration. But what she saw in the slender kid with the sad eyes was utterly beyond Rick. Especially since this whole world might just disappear at any moment. And especially when she could have had him.

The doorchime sounded, and the chief petty officer appeared. "You sent for me, Skipper?"

"That I did, Tucker. You've been telling me about our new ensign's encyclopedic knowledge."

"Aye, Captain. That's right, I have." Tucker shot a worried glance Rick's way.

All Rick could do was shrug in reply. He had no idea what this was about.

"Fine, fine." Captain Arnol seemed entirely at ease, but it was the quiet of a tensely coiled spring. He curled one hand about his steaming mug and said, "I thought you might like to be here for the examination."

Rick froze as all eyes turned his way.

"Draw up a chair, Tucker."

"Aye, aye, Captain." The chief petty officer looked as troubled as Rick felt. "But the lad has only been on board for a few days now."

"I know, I know. But I just wanted to acquaint myself with what you've been talking about." He cast a frosty glance down to the table's end. "The chief petty officer has been telling me that he has yet to come up with a question that you can't answer."

Rick swallowed.

"I was wondering, Ensign, if you would tell our two guests a little about the freighters working the internal Hegemony spaceways."

Petty Officer Tucker did a double take as he glanced down the table and spotted the two scouts. "Skipper, I—"

"Let the lad speak, Tucker," the captain said easily. "What do your friends call you, Ensign?"

"Rick."

"As you have observed, Rick, we like to keep our mess on an informal footing. You can refer to me as Skipper, if you like. That is, unless you have earned my wrath, in which case it would be wise if you did not speak at all."

A ripple of amusement ran down the table. From his previous times at mess, Rick recognized this pattern of questions from the captain as a time-honored tradition. It granted the most junior officers an occasion to speak, when otherwise they would be forced to sit and listen to their seniors dominate the conversation.

Captain Arnol went on, "Now let us see just how far your band of knowledge extends."

Rick found that his throat had suddenly become as dry as cotton. He sipped from his glass, and in that instant felt the knowledge surface. "There are two types of freighters traveling the Hegemony lightways," he replied, wondering if his surprise registered on his face. "The licensed Free Traders and us, the Hegemony's own fleet. We carry all government-issue freight, as well as supplies destined for government bases, outposts, monitor-stations, and Hegemony mining asteroids. We also supply the military. There are private companies who also use our services, especially in some areas."

Arnol nodded. "And why, pray tell, would a private company wish to use us for carrying freight, when the Free Traders are known to be far less expensive?"

"Because the Free Traders avoid the danger zones," Rick replied, and wondered how he could feel so certain about something when he had no idea where it sprang from. "In some areas we are the only vessels that ply the route."

"And what constitutes a danger zone?"

"Three or more vessels lost on a target-route within one Standard year."

"What did I tell you?" Tucker exclaimed. "Not bad for a lad who's never been inbound before in his life."

The captain was less easily impressed. "What reason can you give for these losses?"

The answer, when it came, shocked him so that Rick had difficulty replying. "Pirates."

"What can you tell us about their operations?"

"They are almost impossible to catch, even detect," Rick said, his response slowed by the import of his words. "We know they are active because too many ships have been able to get off final communiques before contact has been lost. Measuring their contact break-points has suggested that they all take place at certain spots along the lightways. Hegemony vessels are beginning to call them strike-points."

Captain Arnol demanded, "Have you been granted access to classified documents?"

"No, Skipper," he replied.

"Then how—" He stopped. "Never mind. You were quite right in your assessment, Tucker."

"Thank you, Skipper," the chief petty officer replied, his barrel chest even more puffed out than usual.

The captain swung his attention back to Rick and demanded, "Have you in your studies ever come across the term shadowlane?"

"Rumors only, Skipper," he replied, gaining strength from the approving looks about the table—especially those of the pretty young assistant signals officer stationed at the room's far end. "It is thought that there might be decommissioned lightways, routes set in the dim recesses of space history."

The captain nodded his approval. "Well done, Rick. You may now breathe easy."

"Thank you, Skipper," he said and permitted himself a grin. Then he caught sight of Consuela's knowing gaze, and for some reason he found the moment losing some of its glory. As though he hadn't earned it. He found himself becoming angry. Maybe the others were right after all. These sensitives just didn't belong.

"Before we move on," the captain said, "do our guests have any questions?"

"I do," Consuela offered. "What is a lightway?"

The power control lieutenant, a sharp-jawed woman whose glances made Rick's skin crawl, snorted her derision. He was not overly sorry when Arnol shifted about and glared her way.

"What is our policy toward honest questions?"

The lieutenant straightened and intoned, "Ignorance in areas other than a shipmate's expertise is excused, and honest questions are welcomed." She shot an angry glance toward the scouts, as though the reprimand were their fault.

"Remember that." He turned his attention to the junior helmswoman, a brilliant former ship's ensign who, according to ship gossip, was slated for bigger things. "Perhaps you would be willing to explain the target-route we follow, Irene."

"Captain," Tucker interrupted, "if you'll not be needing me—"

"Bear with me a moment longer," the captain said, and then to the helmswoman, "Go on."

"Lightways were developed in an earlier spacing era," Irene began. "They are carefully measured routes that the Hegemony established between its major world systems. They run between Hegemony systems and derive their power from the suns to which they are anchored. At the time of their development, ships would power out from an orbital system, accelerating along the lightway, punch through n-space, then decelerate and enter planetary orbit. Lightways are limited in the distance they can cover to twenty-five parsecs, and in earlier times they essentially defined the Hegemony's size. Then you sensitives were discovered, and about the same time the system of vortex transport was developed."

"And now the limits are very different," the captain took over. "Stand down, Irene. Well done."

"Thank you, Skipper."

"Our limits are your limits," Captain Arnol went on, his attention now fully on the scouts. "All Talents are assigned to Starfleet Command, to be trained as pilots or conscripted into the Hegemony's diplomatic service. The number of outbound passenger vessels, scoutships, fleet vessels, and long-haul freighters is limited to the number of pilots. Only a Talent has what it takes to be trained as one. And there are never enough Talents, never enough pilots, never enough communicators, never enough sensitives of any kind. Every post that requires a sensitive is battled over fiercely.

"Controlling Talents has become one of the Starfleet's mightiest tools for holding on to the reigns of power. Which means that an urgent request from some inbound freighter for a pilot to help track down rumors goes unheeded. Three lost vessels per Standard year on certain routes is a small price to pay, when the Hegemony struggles to control outworld regimes with too few ships. The empire is constantly fraying along the edges, and there are never enough sensitives to staff every point. Am I getting through?"

"Yes, Captain," they intoned.

"Not to mention the fact that pilots scorn inbound duty. They consider it beneath them, even when their absence means that I and my ship are in danger every time we traverse a danger zone. Every one of my shipmates has friends who have been lost to the pirates, killed, or sold into slavery. So perhaps you can now understand why your presence is not so welcome."

He dipped a finger in his cup, and drew a straight line

of coffee across the table. He then stabbed the line's midpoint and said, "Many of us have wondered why it is that these pirates attack only at certain points along the lightways. And why our inbound police vessels have had such difficulty in tracking them. What if, we ask, it was because they did not use the lightways at all. What if they had their own routes which only *intersected* ours."

He drew a second diagonal line across the table. "What if they were forced to remain upon their shadowlanes just as we must upon our lightways. We have rumors that this is so."

"Rumors," spat the senior weapons officer. "Rumors and lies and the tales of paid informants who would swear the lost golden moon of Altinthor has appeared above my homeworld, if only I would pay to hear it said."

"Yet rumors are all we have," Captain Arnol replied. "It is said that tribes of thieves have burrowed deep into rogue worlds, sunless balls of ice which in eons past escaped from solar orbit." He moved his cup to one side and leaned across the table. "We and other ships who think there might be something to these rumors have been begging Hegemony for Talents to see if the shadowlanes can be detected. We find nothing suspicious on our instruments, nothing at all. And this is why we who think the rumors might hold truth are opposed by many who think otherwise."

"I for one," the weapons officer said. "The pirates must have learned a way of shielding their ships, nothing more. We know for a fact the slavers have stunners strong enough to break through our shields without cracking our skins. Their cloaking devices are a new technology, nothing more. They stay clear of our detection until they attack, and they attack only when we're too far from help." He looked scornfully across at the pair. "I for one say keep the sensitives off our ship, and good riddance to the lot of them. What we need is to stop spending time on these overbred overspoiled prima donnas and build ourselves better ships with more powerful weapons."

Rick nodded his agreement. That made sense to him. The guy sounded like his coach giving the same pre-season speech year after year—strive for strength, sweat for guts, go for glory. Besides, maybe this would wipe that superior attitude off Consuela's face.

The senior weapons officer's gaze flickered in Rick's direction, but all he said was, "We don't need to analyze these pirates, Captain. We need to have Starfleet build us better weapons so we can blast them out of the sky."

The captain calmly waited until the senior weapons officer was through, then said, "Any officer on this ship is welcome to voice his or her opinion at mess, as long as the captain's decision is fully obeyed and his orders willingly carried out. Is that clear?"

"Aye, aye, Skipper," came the growled reply.

"Very well. Now tell us what you felt at the zero mark, Scout."

"Like a hundred metal fingers were digging under my skin," Wander replied.

"It was horrible," Consuela agreed.

The captain turned and gave the senior weapons officer a very long look. Then he asked, "Signals, when is our next suspected strike point?"

"Three hours, plus or minus."

"Scouts, I cannot order you to stand another watch," the captain said, his eyes still locked with the weapons officer's. "But I would ask you. Could you endure the experience again?"

Wander exchanged glances with Consuela, then replied for them both, "If it would help the ship."

"It might," the captain replied. "It very well might." He released the weapons officer and turned to the chief petty officer. "Do you see why I asked you to stay, Tucker?"

"Yes, Skipper," the burly man replied, his astonished gaze flickering back and forth across the table.

"See that word spreads through the crew. Let them know we have a couple of Talents who are standing double watch to help us out."

"They won't believe it."

"Perhaps not. But it may give them pause before making trouble." To the pair he said, "Watch yourselves between decks. I am hereby ordering all my officers to assist you, and granting you full access to the officers' quarters. You are also granted temporary pilot's status on the flight deck, which means you may come and go as you please."

"Thank you, Captain," Wander replied, the exultation clear in his voice.

"Skipper," the senior weapons officer interrupted. "I'd be willing to take the ensign here under my wing for a spell."

That brought a smile to Captain Arnol's face. "This is indeed a mess to remember. Does the offer pass muster with you, Tucker?"

"It's a bit early in the game, Skipper, but as I've said, this lad shows all the makings of a good officer."

"Very well, I approve." The captain turned to Rick and said, "You should know, Ensign, that you are being accorded quite an honor. First of all, Chief Petty Officer Tucker is known through the Hegemony as a tough taskmaster, and he's had nothing but praise for you—something that has little to do with your book learning."

"Thank you, Captain," Rick said, glorying in the fact that Consuela was there to hear it.

"And secondly, this is the first time in my memory that

our senior weapons officer has volunteered to work with any ensign on this ship. He is known as the best marksman riding the inbound lightways, and I am constantly fighting off attempts by other ships to lure him away. You will do well to listen with care and obey with alacrity."

"Aye, aye, Skipper."

Arnol glanced at the wall chronolog and rose to his feet. "All but those whose watch begins now are dismissed until T minus fifteen minutes."

–Fourteen–

"I take it you don't have any more time for these sensitives than I do."

"No, Senior Weapons Officer."

"Call me Guns." The senior weapons officer marched down the passage with all the grace of an impatient bull. He was not a big man, but Rick would not want to tangle with him. Muscles corded up taut under every square inch of exposed skin. His knuckles were as knotted as gravel, his nose looked twice broken, and a pouch of scar tissue split his left eyebrow. Guns was a man who liked to fight, with or without his weapons. "Sensitives, pah! Wouldn't give a barrel full of space for the whole lot of them. They can't even sit in a powered chair, you know. Saw it happen once when I was about your age. Novice sat down without disconnecting, the skipper powered up for takeoff, and next thing anybody knew the sensitive was fried. Wouldn't shed a tear if it happened to the whole lot of them."

Rick felt as though he were barely touching the deck. He was still junior officer on the ship, but here he was, being treated like one of the crew. It reminded him of how he had felt when he had finally made the varsity team.

There were still vague whispers circulating through his mind and heart, questioning where he was and what he knew. But this place was real. He no longer doubted that. Real as anything he had left behind. He could not explain what was going on, and to be honest was caring less and less about the hows and whys with each passing hour. The challenge was great, the action fast, the opportunities tremendous.

Rick was having the time of his life.

The senior weapons officer cast him a canny glance. "You look like a fighter to me, lad. Am I right?"

"There was a sport I played before—" Rick stopped and corrected himself, "Back home. It was called a contact sport, but it was really a stylized battle. I loved it."

"Thought so," Guns said. "Others mighta been fooled by that pretty face of yours, but I know a warrior when I see one."

A *warrior*. Rick thrilled to the sound. "I really appreciate your giving me a chance."

"Earn the privilege," Guns replied. "Do well and make me proud."

The flight deck was structured as four pyramids of platforms set like great steps. Chromed railings and curved flight consoles separated each dais. The captain's chair stood isolated upon the central and highest dais. Before and below him were the helmsmen's three chairs. Engine, Power, and Signals rested on the three other pyramid bases, curving embankments interconnected by joined consoles like petals of three flowers grown together into one. At the crest of the signals platform was the pilot's chair. At the top of the power pyramid stood the weapons console.

Guns relieved the duty officer, then maneuvered the dais' second chair up close to his own, clamped it down, and flicked the power switch. "You won't be sleeping much these next few weeks," he warned. "I'll be expecting you to spend your off-duty hours on your hands and knees, getting to know our weapons better than your mother knew your father."

"I can do without sleep, Guns."

"That's the spirit. I'll be assigning you a gunner's mate who'll walk you through the lovelies. You'll come to know them by name, or I'll know the reason why." He pointed at the two arm-consoles and the three-tiered structure, which could be raised over the chairback. "Next few days we'll do some dry-firing runs, let you get a feel for the triggers. But first we've got to see if there's a match here."

Consuela and Wander chose that moment to enter the flight deck. Although she did not look his way, Rick found himself acutely aware of her presence. She spoke to Wander in the low tones of two people concerned only with each other. He found himself growing hot with anger.

Guns noticed his reaction, glanced over, and grunted, "Aye, they get under my skin too. But they've got the captain's blessing, so you'll do well to ignore them. Arnol's not a man to brook an officer going against his bidding." He patted the arm of Rick's chair. "Now set yourself down."

The chair conformed to Rick's contours as he settled, then extended two bands that Guns pulled up across his shoulders and fastened to the chairback. "We don't normally bother with the straps unless we're on alert."

"What are they for?"

"You'll see." He settled into his own chair. "Weapons can't be learned from a book. Either you've got what it takes to be a gunnery officer, or you don't. Ready?"

Rick shrugged as far as the shoulder straps would allow. "I guess so."

"Watch my actions." He keyed in his console. "Green light for all systems. But they're separate. We call this resting at arms. Standard ops for non-alert."

"What do you mean, separate?"

Instead of replying, Guns flipped his comm switch and demanded, "If that was a snore I just heard, I'll have you swabbing down the outer hull while we're under power."

"No need to talk that way, Guns," came back the laconic reply. "You know I don't snore."

"That you, Simmer?"

"Now who else would it be, this watch?"

"I'm taking a new boy through a dry run. Stand by with power."

"Power standing by," came the droned response. "Hope you singe his eyebrows for waking me up."

"What should I call you, Ensign?"

"Rick."

"All right, Rick. Grab hold of your socks." With both hands Guns pushed up two parallel series of levers. Rick gripped his armrests in an uncontrollable spasm as the power flooded in. But it was not power as he had known in the ensign's duty chair. This was power with focus. Power with purpose. Power with *menace*.

His awareness coursed through the ship, directed by the instruments under Guns' control toward the four great chambers flanking the ship's thrusters. The weapons were situated beside the thrusters, he realized, because they drew from the same power source. Shield, thruster, and weapons, all powered by the same miniature star burning fiercely at the ship's heart.

"Shield," Guns said softly, and Rick could scarcely see his hand touch the controls. He was drawn inexorably out to the force-field that surrounded the ship, watched it mount from standard power to full attack status, and felt the power surge through himself as well. He *felt* it.

"Tracking systems," Guns intoned, and Rick felt himself

connect to the signals station, then move outward, sniffing the boundaries of space for incoming threats, anything that he could fasten onto and attack.

"Weapons," Guns said, and Rick bucked against the straps as the spasm locked his muscles. The power was *enormous*. The dampers were lifted, and a shining arm of the ship's star reached out to awaken the dormant might. Rick felt the same strength course through his own limbs, and he wanted to roar with the primeval lust for battle. He was no longer a puny human, formed of mere flesh and bone. He was a warrior knight of old, encased in battle armor, shielded and armed and *ready*.

"Enough," Guns said, and swept the levers back toward him.

The power and the image faded. "What did you do that for?"

Guns inspected him carefully, then nodded. "Just as I thought," he said approvingly. "I've got myself a natural on my hands."

But Rick was not ready to let it go. "Can't you just—"

"One step at a time, lad. One step at a time." The weapons officer flicked the console to standby. "Release yourself from the straps and go fetch me a mug of coffee. You'll find the makings in the alcove beside the portal."

Rick fumbled for the catches, then raised himself with difficulty. His legs were as weak as after the first practice of the season. But the sensation of power stayed with him. He walked to the alcove, surrounded by the mantle of force that he had at his command.

A dulcet voice behind him asked, "How is Guns treating you?"

Rick turned to find himself facing the assistant signals officer, an auburn-haired beauty whose feminine form could not be disguised by the austere uniform. "That was the most incredible thing I've ever known in my life."

She smiled with eyes the same burnished shade as her hair. "Maybe we could meet after watch and you can tell me about it."

The surging might awakened by the weapons system took on a different focus. Rick felt his entire being vibrating with the strength of his desire. It enflamed him. "I'd like that," he said, his voice as shaky as his legs. "Very much."

The young woman noted the change with a welcoming smile. "I'll come by your cabin," she said softly, and turned away.

When Rick returned to the weapons station, Guns accepted his mug and said, "She's a pretty young thing, that one."

Rick slumped back down in his chair and mumbled, "Don't tell me that's off limits."

"You are ordered to keep up with your duties and learn the weapons systems backward and forward. If you've still got the strength to do anything besides sleep after that, then what you do off watch is nobody's business but your own." The weapons officer took a sip, then grinned, exposing teeth worn to flat stumps by constant grinding. "Gunnies have a reputation to uphold on and off the flight deck, Ensign. Remember that."

"Ten minutes to transition," droned the helmsman.

Wander watched her settle into the chair beside him, and asked, "Did you notice how it felt with the amp on before we hit the shadowlane?"

"As if I were expanding," Consuela replied. She picked up her headset and fitted it on. No one paid them any attention. The countdown to null-space transition kept everyone on the flight deck fully occupied.

"Right. That was less than one-tenth power, and with the headset damping mechanism on full." Wander scanned the flight deck. "But there won't be any noise here on the sensitive level until after we make transition."

"So?"

"So I'd like to try out the amp without the damping mechanism, and then stay hooked on while we make the passage through n-space."

"Do you think that's wise?"

He shrugged. "It's the first time I've ever been in a ship, and the first time I've been someplace where it's *quiet*. I want to try out this amping system, see what it does. How else am I going to learn how to guide a starship through uncharted null-space?"

Consuela thought it over and decided, "Then I want to do it with you."

He grinned. "I was hoping you'd say that."

"Then we'd better hurry." She fitted on her headset. "One tiny bit of power at a time, okay?"

"Don't worry." He unfastened the damping box from both their headsets, fitted his headset to his temples, and switched on the pilot's console. "If you start feeling anything unpleasant, tell me and I'll power down. Ready?"

She settled back in her chair. "Yes."

"Here goes." He nudged the amp dial.

"Oh, my." Immediately her senses were extended to the ship and beyond.

Wander turned the dial back to zero just as the helmsman chanted the five-minute call. "That was pretty strong, wasn't it?"

"How much did you give us?"

"Less than one percent."

She gaped. "The dial goes to one hundred?"

"Look for yourself." He leaned out of the way so she

could see. "The normal range runs up to sixty percent. The top portion is what Senior Pilot Grimson called the Stellar range, that's handled by the override here. Then there's the redline." He traced a finger around the stable control meter. "You have to remember, this was developed to work with sensitives who don't hear *anything* without being hooked up to the amp. I've never seen directions for how it works with a Talent."

"Two minutes," intoned the helmsman.

"What do you think we should do?"

He thought it over. "Let's take it one step at a time. This first transition, we'll stay undamped but with no amp power, and see how we feel. Maybe go a little higher on the next transition, and see if we can chart our way."

The captain completed his final station-by-station check just as the helmsman began chanting down the seconds. Despite Wander's calm confidence, Consuela felt a thrill of nerves. "I wish I could hold your hand."

Reluctantly Wander shook his head. "I don't think that'd be a good idea. Not on the flight deck."

"Ten," chanted the helmsman. "Nine, eight, seven, six . . ."

And then time began to slow.

Gradually her attention was stretched in two, a physical portion linked to the steady chanting, and a mental which began to slow and stretch like taffy. Except for Wander's calm presence there beside her, she would have been terrified.

The ship continued along the carefully charted and computed course, barreling down the lightway, increasing speed at a steady rate until the final second, the final nudge, and the instantaneous push through null-space. Beyond time, beyond physical reality, in and out in the span of no time at all, not even a microsecond.

Yet there had been something. Between the elastic final second and the return to the first stretched second after transition, her sense of awareness moved beyond the vastness of space. There was an instant beyond time, and at that point something called to her at the very deepest level. Something so powerful and yet so comforting that sensing it created an answering voice in her heart. A soundless, wordless keening, a yearning for that which she somehow felt she had known all along, yet never truly known. Something she had lost, yet never had.

The helmsman's chant began counting back up the seconds, the power officer intoned the gradual braking reduction in force, and little by little the sense of physical time and mental time meshed back together for her. Wander rose unsteadily to his feet. His voice trembled slightly as he said, "I need a break."

Consuela needed both hands to pull off her headset. "Did you hear it?"

"I'm not sure what I heard," he replied and pushed himself to his feet. "Let me take a moment's rest, then we'll talk."

–Fifteen–

"I don't like it," Consuela whispered. "It's too danger-ous."

"Less dangerous than the ship going into a possible strike-point cold," Wander replied. "The captain has al-ready said he's going to place the ship on full alert. All they have to go on are a couple of ships that disappeared be-tween standard communication checks."

They had been arguing since transition. Wander's idea was to try to extend their awareness beyond the ship, and see if the shadowlane could be identified in advance. Knowing Wander was right did not make it any easier to accept. "But what if—"

"You know we're going to try," Wander told her, settling into his seat. "We can keep arguing, or we can just go ahead and start."

His calm resolve robbed her of the will to resist. She set-tled into her own chair, said, "Promise me you'll take it easy."

"The first sign of trouble," he assured her, "and we re-treat immediately."

The flight deck was quiet, each station staffed by only

one crewman. But it was a tense calm, a time of waiting. The fifteen-minute checks were done with voices clipped and strained by what all knew lay ahead.

"That transition reminded me of something. When I was little," she began, then hesitated, caught by the look he gave her as he turned from his controls. "What is it?"

"That is the first time you have spoken of your childhood," he said. "Go on. What happened?"

"I had a friend named Daniel," she started, then hesitated, wondering how and what to say. "He would pray with me. Sometimes I had a sense of being connected with, I don't know, something *beyond*. But as I grew older I thought it was childish, something I needed to put aside. Now I'm not so sure."

Wander watched her for a moment, then said softly, "I would like to know all about when you were young."

"It was not a happy time."

"No," he said, his eyes deepening with compassion. "Perhaps that's why it seems so special to share the memories."

She reached over, squeezed his hand, not caring who noticed or what they thought. Her heart was simply too full to let the moment go without some act of sharing.

He let the moment linger, a bond growing between them, then finally said, "Ready to start?"

"If you are."

"Okay." Reluctantly he released her hand, turned back to the dials, said, "We will take this one small step at a time."

Consuela adjusted her headset, leaned back, and sighed as the power began surging, granting her that sense of expansion. With the first nudge of power, she felt her awareness pushed beyond the flight deck to encompass the entire ship. Not touching anything, not belonging anywhere. Another notch up the power-scale, and she felt herself extending beyond the ship itself, moving into the toneless depths of neighboring space. Another nudge, and she grew able to travel up and down the lightway, moving ahead of the ship, watching back behind, holding on to the security of her chair, feeling the ship anchoring her physically as her heightened senses reached out farther and farther.

"Can you hear me?" Wander whispered.

"Yes."

"Do you want to go on?"

"Maybe just a little."

A fourth nudge, and she found herself better able to focus if she closed her eyes. A fifth, and she knew if she wanted she could alter her mental course and begin searching space in every direction. She did not reach out. She could not. It was hard enough to remain anchored in the speeding ship, her attention stretched outward along the lightway, without reaching through the vastness of empty space. She was afraid if she moved too far from the lightway's established path she might never find her way home.

A sixth, and her awareness shot forward, flying past the upcoming shadowlane so fast that there was no time to react to the scathing glance. A seventh nudge, and she became aware of something else. Something *more*.

"There isn't anything I can teach this lad," Simmers announced to the senior weapons officer. Simmers was a lanky gunner's mate whose laconic air belied a mind as sharp as a knife.

In their first few moments together, Rick had quickly surmised that he loved his machines and would brook no slacking when it came to learning the tasks at hand. Which made the sudden appearance of the required knowledge that much more pleasing.

"He musta memorized the entire ship's weapons manuals," Simmers reported. "Even knew the wiring and circuitry patterns."

Guns bore down hard on Rick. "You told me the truth about your background?"

"Yes, Senior Weapons Officer."

"Never seen anything like it in all my born days," Simmers declared.

"I have ways of checking this out," Guns warned. "Changing your name won't help you in the end."

"I've never spaced before in my life, honest," Rick said.

"We'll see about that," he growled. Then his gaze flickered to the other side of the flight deck. "What's this, what's this?"

Rick turned to see Captain Arnol climb to the pilot's dais and lean against the console as Wander spoke low and urgently.

"Those the sensitives Tucker was going on about?" Simmers asked quietly.

"Aye, and there's trouble a'brewing, you can bet your back teeth on that," Guns rumbled. "Wonder what mischief they're scheming up over there."

The captain turned to the front of the flight deck and said, "Signals, what's our T minus?"

"Ninety-one minutes and counting, Skipper."

"And beyond that?"

The junior signals officer coded in her console, then replied, "A questionable strike-point a half-parsec beyond. One freighter missing and presumed, two Standards ago."

"Travel time?"

"Seventy-five minutes beyond the next strike-point."

The captain turned back to Wander and demanded harshly, "That it?"

"It must be," Wander replied.

Consuela nodded agreement. "The distances fit."

"Are you sure?"

Wander hesitated. "No, Captain. But I think this is real."

"You can't expect me to throw the entire ship into a panic because of a guess, Scout," Arnol snapped.

"Just as I said," Guns muttered. "Trouble's on the rise."

"Captain, it's all too new for me to say for certain what—"

"Well, I can," Consuela declared defiantly. "Two of us can't be totally wrong. It's definitely another shadowlane."

Rick watched the captain glare at her, but she refused to back down. His eyes still on Consuela, he snapped, "Helmsman!"

"Yes, Captain."

"Inform the chief petty officer that the ship is to move onto full combat footing."

An electric current shot through the flight deck. The captain wheeled about and demanded, "Guns, who is on weapons station duty?"

"I am, Captain," Simmers replied.

The captain frowned. "What are you doing away from your station, mister?"

"I ordered him up to flight deck, Skipper," Guns replied. "We're planning the lad's training."

"Training will have to wait. Are we ready for full power to all weaponry?"

"Aye, Captain," Guns replied. "I ran through the gamut myself not two hours ago."

"Very well. Simmers, you have precisely ten seconds to return to your station and prepare for attack mode."

"Mind if I ask what's amiss, Skipper?" Guns asked.

"The scouts have detected another shadowlane," Captain Arnol replied, speaking to the flight deck as a whole. "And a third beyond that. They claim there's activity on the third lane, and well within cannon range."

"Pirates?" Guns said doubtfully and glared at the scouts. "Skipper, do you really think these novices can be trusted—"

"Don't bother me with questions I can't answer, Guns. Simmers, you have your orders. Helmsman!"

"Chief Petty Officer Tucker has been informed, sir."

"Very well." The captain hesitated long enough to cast another glance toward his scouts, then said, "All crew, stand by for action stations. This vessel will enter red alert status in two hours. Mark!"

"Red alert, one-twenty minutes and counting," intoned the helmsman.

"All senior officers to my cabin in fifteen minutes." Arnol focused on the scouts and said ominously, "You had better be right."

Curiously, neither Consuela nor Wander felt ensnared by the feverish excitement that captured the rest of the ship. Consuela willingly accepted Wander's suggestion that they return to his cabin until they approached the next shadowlane. The passages were filled with crew who went hurtling by, pausing only to flash an incredulous glance their way. Word had already spread throughout the vessel. Two young scouts, utter novices to space, claimed to have detected a new shadowlane. The same shadowlanes which, up to now, had been little more than speculation. They also claimed to have identified pirates lying in wait. The same pirates who, up to now, had been little more than rumors. And on the basis of their unsubstantiated claims, the captain had ordered the ship to be readied for combat.

"Hey, youngsters!" A gray-headed swabbie stopped them with an upraised hand. He had the look of a veteran tomcat, scarred and beat up and still full of life. "This challenge for real?"

"We think so," Wander replied.

"We know so," Consuela corrected. "Something's out there where it shouldn't be. Whether it's a pirate or not, your guess is as good as mine."

"Ain't nothing else could be hanging about in the middle of deep space," the swabbie replied and eyed them shrewdly. "They's laying ten-to-one odds that you're wrong and the whole thing ain't nothing but smoke. Think I should take some of that?"

Consuela grinned and replied, "Bet your back teeth."

The swabbie laughed and slapped his thigh. "Gal, I like your spirit. Anybody on lower decks tries to make trouble, you come find old Tinker."

"Thank you, Tinker," Consuela said, putting as much feeling as she could into the words. "It's good to know we have friends like you."

Ancient eyes sparked with pleasure. "Aye, missie, friend it is. Like I say, any of these swabbies stand in your way, give me a shout. We'll fix 'em good."

As he keyed open his door, Wander asked, "What was that all about?"

"Oh, he reminded me of some of the geezers back in my old neighborhood." She eased her neck muscles. "Now that we're off the deck, I really feel tired."

"Me too." Wander called for chair and bed. "You can lie down, if you like."

"Come sit down beside me," she said, settling down and patting the mattress. "I need to tell you something."

"I think I know," Wander said.

"You can't. It's not possible." Suddenly she was nervous. Not so much about his reaction. Wander was the most accepting person she had ever met. But bringing it up forced her also to consider beyond the moment. To face the threat of tomorrow.

"You don't come from an outworld," Wander said quietly, his eyes returning to the sorrow of earlier days. Days before they had met. "Not the way we think of it."

She showed her astonishment. "How did you know?"

"I've been thinking a lot about it," he said. "Little things keep coming up, things even an outworlder had to know. And something else. It wasn't until I was here alone after takeoff that I realized what had bothered me about that night when we met on the field." He looked at her. "There was only one set of footsteps in the snow coming out from the port."

"I wanted to tell you," she said. "From the very first moment. I just didn't know how."

He took her hand in both of his. "Tell me now."

– Sixteen –

Rick thought it felt a lot like the run-up to a big game.

He sat in the far corner of the weapons platform, grateful for the chance to stay and take part. He was almost completely ignored. The first team had been called in. Guns manned the primary console, his numbers two and three tucked in to either side. Rick's chair was squeezed up to the back railing, but he didn't mind—he was still able to sit and feel a part of the rising tide of tense waiting.

Then Wander and Consuela returned, and Rick found himself minding very much.

The entire flight deck turned, and all activity stopped momentarily as attention focused on the pair who had brought them to ready status.

"I believe we have a countdown to red alert," the captain barked, and activity resumed. But attention was continually cast their way.

Rick found himself reaching a slow burn. He wasn't used to being sidelined while someone else played the star.

He watched movement slow once more as the next shadowlane was approached. He saw the pair huddle together, as though drawing support from one another, although only Wander wore the headset. Rick heard Signals chant down the seconds to the next possible shadowlane. He and all the flight-deck crew saw a shudder rack both Wander and Consuela.

Rick watched Wander struggle to push off the after-effects, then announce, "It's another one, Captain."

The captain snapped, "Mark!"

Signals responded, "Right on target again, Skipper."

The flight deck responded with a murmur of astonishment, which only the senior weapons officer and his crew did not share. "Aye, all right for some," Guns muttered and coursed his stubby fingers across the weapons console. "But it takes guts to handle *real* power."

From his central station, Captain Arnol asked the scouts, "Can you still function?"

"I can," Consuela said quietly, and stilled Wander's protest with a hand on his arm. "I didn't wear the headset. You did. Let me check."

"But I can't monitor," he protested.

"You don't have to listen in to set the amp level." Consuela slipped on her headset, settled back and said, "Ready."

An electric stillness on the flight deck settled as Consuela closed her eyes and frowned in concentration.

Rick whispered to no one in particular, "What is she doing?"

"Listening to space," Guns muttered back. "Aye, takes a vacuum between the ears to do it, too."

Rick turned to the veteran. "Why don't you like them?"

"You haven't been around like I have," Guns replied, his gaze leveled like a missile tracker on the pair. "Having a pilot on the flight deck is like taking a plague on board."

Consuela opened her eyes, struggled to focus, and announced, "They're still there, Captain."

"You're sure?"

"I can't say what they are," she replied, her voice quiet yet confident. "But there is definitely a ship waiting down the next shadowlane."

"Any ship in this quadrant that is standing poised off a lightway can be presumed to be enemy." He turned to the lower deck. "Any communication traffic?"

"Nothing in the sector at all except our vessel and the port," Signals replied.

He turned back to Consuela. "How far off the lightway are they lying?"

When she hesitated, Wander replied for her, "About two minutes at our present speed."

"Guns?"

"Aye, Skipper," the veteran groused. "Well within stunner range."

"Very well." He keyed his own console. "Chief Petty Officer, is the ship ready?"

"Battened down tight, Captain." The flight deck's intercom carried Tucker's bundled agitation loud and clear. "The crew's raring to go."

"Very well." He keyed a second switch and said, "All hands, this is the captain speaking. An unidentified vessel has been tentatively identified lying off the lightway approximately"—he checked his console—"forty minutes ahead of us. No communication traffic has been detected. According to Hegemony law, a vessel not directly upon a lightway and not sounding a distress call may be assumed to be enemy and fired upon. In the case that the vessel is a slaver and this ship is hit by stunners, all crew are ordered to remain suited and shielded, with arms at the ready, until the all-clear is sounded. Marine units, prepare for possible boarding. Good luck and good hunting. Captain out."

He looked down at the upturned faces before him, hesitated a long moment, then nodded. "Hit it."

A thrumming tone sounded over the ship's intercom. "Battle stations. Battle stations." The signals officer droned the words, yet nothing could keep the excitement from spilling over. "This ship is now on red alert. Battle stations."

"I want you scouts to check the vessel every five minutes," he ordered. "Alert me immediately to any change in status."

"Aye, aye, Captain." Wander slipped on his headset.

The captain swung around. "Guns, I have decided to go ahead as discussed in my quarters."

"But, Skipper—"

"You will not raise the shields," he ordered, overriding his weapons officer. "You will arm yourself, but you will not draw your weapons."

"I have to protest," Guns replied. "That puts us at a desperate disadvantage."

But Arnol was not finished. "You will track at your absolute limits. You will hold yourself fully ready to draw and strike. At the first forward move, you will attack. You will not wait for my command. I want you to try to take out their shields without cracking their skin." He let the orders sink in, then continued. "I wouldn't dare try this maneuver with anybody less skilled than you, Guns. Think you're up to it?"

Clearly the captain had hit the correct key. The weapons officer swelled visibly. "Give it our best shot, Skipper."

"Cripple an attack vessel, but leave those aboard alive." The captain swung about to ensure that the entire flight deck's attention was turned toward the weapons station. "I've never heard of such a maneuver."

"Aye, it'd be one for the books, that's a fact," Guns replied, basking in the attention.

"I ask this only because no one has ever captured a pirate vessel."

"Always wanted to be a bit of history in the making, Skipper."

"You realize, of course," the captain went on, "we are placing this ship and the lives of all within her in your hands."

"Split-second timing," Guns replied, planning out loud. "Blast her shield, hit them with a stunner bolt, melt the guts of her weaponry, go for the drive system. A four-step attack faster than you can blink your eye. That's the ticket."

"Very well, Guns, you have convinced me. I hereby authorize you to fire at will. But if the plan does not appear to work at first blow, I want you to annihilate her, is that clear? No time for inspection or hesitation, man. The risk is too great."

"The instant it even appears that they might have either drive or secondary weapons," Guns promised, "that vessel will disappear, Captain. Mark my words."

Captain Arnol's features were more sharply drawn than ever. He nodded his acceptance and ordered, "To your weapons, then."

–Seventeen–

Weapons Lieutenant Valens was a taciturn young man with the slender yet muscular build of a gymnast. He had done little more than nod in Rick's direction since arriving. When Guns swiveled back around to his console, however, he asked, "You want a trainee up here in the middle of a fight?"

Guns glanced in Rick's direction, hesitated, and for an agonizing instant Rick thought he was going to be taken out of the action.

The senior weapons officer caught a hint of Rick's distress, and humor flickered across his features. "Not just yet."

The lieutenant shrugged, as though it was of no great concern. "Might get awful busy later."

"Maybe our Rick here might serve a purpose."

"A trainee?"

"The boy's a natural, mark my words." Guns mulled it over for a long moment, then turned to his number three, a long-time weapons officer who clearly was not concerned with rising farther up the ladder of authority. "How'd you like to arm a second ferret?"

Experienced eyes cast themselves over Rick's form. "You really think he's got what it takes?"

"Set him on the power bank, have him hunt with our secondary weapons. Never can tell, an unknown vessel might have a little derringer up its sleeve." Guns nodded at the sound of his own decision. "I'll take the shield, that's the trickiest bit because I'll have to give it a glancing blow. Straight shot might leave us with a cloud of nuts and bolts."

"I'll hit them with a stun bolt soon as the shields are down," the number three offered. "Then go for the drive tubes."

"I'll take weapons," Lieutenant Valens said.

"Aim well back," Guns ordered. "Stay clear of the upper decks. I'll put a second shot on the nose and take out their control systems soon as the shield's cracked."

"You sure it's wise to leave a novice on the deck during action?" Valens asked once more, his gaze coming nowhere near Rick.

"Can't hurt," Guns replied. Clearly his mind was made up. "We three are seeing to all the known targets. Let him hunt about on his own, play the extra ferret. Lad's got to have his first taste of battle sometime."

Rick felt his entire system drenched in adrenaline when the two assistant gunners nodded their acceptance. "Thanks, Guns."

"Make me proud, lad," the grizzled veteran replied, understanding him fully.

Rick searched his memory, and when nothing came up he decided he had to ask. "What's a ferret?"

The officers exchanged glances, and the number three accepted with a slight nod. "It's what we call a tracker in hunt-attack mode," he replied, as the other two bent over the weapons console. "You heard the captain give us the right to fire at will?"

"Yes."

"This means that as soon as the target is identified, we attack. Weapons officers assigned as ferrets search for unexpected threats." He motioned to Rick's overhead console. "Draw down your systems console and code in."

Instantly Rick knew what was required. He keyed the lever situated at the end of his right chair arm, and the console smoothly swung up and over and into place at chest level. A second key drew up the two side consoles, so that he was now situated at the center of an electronic cocoon. He scanned the elaborate array and felt the sweep of sudden understanding rise with the tide of his mounting excitement. The checklist was there, ready and waiting in his mind. He poised his hands over the incredibly complex pattern of levers and keys and readouts, and began. As his hands moved, he vocalized, "Connectors keyed and coded."

"Power up."

He reached for the central dials and with both hands swept the levers forward. "Powering." As the levers rose, so too did the soaring sense of reaching out, joining with a force of incredible magnitude. "Power at full and holding."

The lieutenant paused in his work long enough to glance Rick's way. He then turned to Guns and raised an eyebrow.

"What did I tell you?" Guns replied proudly.

"Power to tracking," Valens ordered.

The side consoles were his tracking units, intended to be set in motion, then followed with gentle nudges of the two control sticks rising from their flexible mountings at hand level. Rick directed the power now set at his control to both tracking mechanisms. "Tracking alerted."

"Ready your weapons."

The top-central console drawn down over his head was his weaponry. Phasers, neutron missiles, strafers, stun bolts—they and the close-hold defenders called energy lances could at the press of keys be armed and directed to his control sticks. Tracking would be guided and locked, then with a press of the red-light buttons capping his control sticks, the weapons would be fired. Rick ran through the weapons-power keys, then intoned as calmly as his quaking chest would permit, "Request weapons arming code."

"Listen to the lad," Guns exclaimed, turning to give Rick his flat-toothed grin. "How does it feel?"

"Incredible," he said, willing his hands to remain steady.

"Know what it is that's firing the flame in your gut?" The weapons officer's eyes held a knowing gleam. "It's the coming battle, lad. You can *smell* it, can't you?"

"I think so," he said, and could not help but grin so hugely it felt as though his face were splitting. "Thanks for letting me stay, Guns. Don't worry, I won't let you down."

The veteran laughed and slapped the boy's shoulder. "That you won't, lad. That you won't. I'll be holding your final controls in my hands, mind, so there won't be any chance of firing early." He nodded to his number three. "Code his arms. Let the lad flex his muscles."

"Coding in."

Something caught the weapons officer's eye, and the vast good humor slipped from his face. "Just look at those two over there, would you," Guns muttered. "Their heads together, practicing their mumbo-jumbo. Who'd have thought the captain would place a ship of the line in the hands of two novices like that."

Without looking up from his own monitors, Lieutenant Valens replied, "At least they've given us a chance to fight. You've got to grant them that."

"I'll grant them nothing," came the growled reply.

"Witches is all they are. Witches and wizards run this Hegemony. It's a sad day when real men have got to bow and scrape to the likes of them."

Rick took advantage of the companionable atmosphere and asked, "What happened to you?"

Guns swung his way. "Eh?"

"Why are you so bitter about sensitives?"

There was a moment of grinding teeth before Guns muttered, "When I first started spacing I came up against a monster in midnight robes. A pilot who didn't like my attitude. Kept me a midshipman on a moon bus for five stinking years before I could shake off his curse and prove my worth. Five years I lost because I refused to suck up to the pompous fool."

Rick ventured, "Maybe those two are different."

All three weapons officers turned his way. Guns demanded, "What's it to you, then? You fancy the lass?"

"Not at all," he protested. Under the veteran's fiery gaze he confessed, "I knew her back home, that's all."

"You're both from the same homeworld?"

"Same town."

"Is that a fact." He looked bemusedly back toward the pilot's station. "I always figured them to have sprung up full blown from under rocks, like other vermin."

The lieutenant snorted a laugh but did not speak up.

"Stay away from them, lad," Guns warned. "You've got the makings of a top-flight officer. Don't let their kind destroy your chances like they did mine. Not a sensitive's been born that wasn't pure poison to good and decent folk."

–Eighteen–

To Consuela's great relief, she and Wander were left alone, an island of calm in a turbulent sea. With each five-minute course mark from signals and the helmsman, the flight deck's frenetic pace rose one notch. Yet the two of them remained isolated on the pilot's station, separated by an immeasurable gulf from the remainder of the flight deck.

Each five minutes also meant reaching out, connecting with the approaching shadowlane, following its course and touching briefly upon the silent vessel. It was a harrowing experience.

The shadowlane vibrated with a power that was as forboding as it was dark, a nemesis that left them feeling unclean. The closer they drew, the less amplification it required to reach forward and monitor, and the stronger the brooding menace sounded in their minds. It was an infernal buzzing, a hissing of unclean energies that tainted their innermost beings.

Evil.

They traded off the monitoring duties, one reaching outward every five minutes while the other leaned close and gave comfort. Consuela did not know which was worse, having to sit and watch Wander flinch as he drew into contact or doing so herself.

"Twenty minutes and counting," intoned Signals.

"Status unchanged," responded Wander, peeling the headset from his temples and discarding it upon the console. To Consuela he murmured, "I'm down to amp level five."

"We know what to look for," she agreed.

He nodded. "It's strange. When I'm out there, I can feel you."

"I know," she said, wishing she could touch him. "Just knowing your love is there with me—" She stopped with the sudden realization of what she had said.

He turned to her, his gaze soft and full and deep. "My love," he whispered.

She felt a swelling pressure push up from her chest and lock her throat tight. "I'm so scared."

"Not about the threat up ahead."

"No." She willed herself to steady. "Thank you for believing my story."

His brown eyes were great pools of yearning. "How long can you stay?"

"I don't know. It's the hardest part of all, not knowing."

"Do you want to leave?"

"No," she said, definite now. "I think of home, I wonder how my mother is. But my place is here now." She had to stop and swallow. "With you."

They sat in silent sharing until the monitor chimed.

Wander said, "Let me do it this time."

"No." She stopped further argument by fitting on her headset. "All right. Amp up."

Reluctantly he acquiesced. "I'll go to four unless you say more."

"I'll be fast," she said, and as the amp level rose, she reached outward, a tightly focused beam of concentration, racing down the lightway, unfettered by time or physical bonds. The shadowlane appeared and she veered off, anchoring herself to the lightway as she searched down the unclean way, feeling the buzzing vibratory patterns course through her mind. She flitted to the darkened vessel, saw it holding to its stationary pattern, and returned in a flash.

Yet even at her rapid and focused pace, she could not deny what she almost heard.

"Fifteen minutes and counting," droned Signals.

"Status unchanged," she replied, setting down her headset.

Wander asked. "Are you all right?"

She nodded. "I'll be glad when this is over."

"Me too."

She looked up and out at the star-flecked expanse. In the far right corner, a nebulous gas cloud extended one purple-flecked tentacle out over a thousand stars. A supernova blazed almost directly overhead, outshining the two galaxy swarms that flanked it. "I wish I knew I could stay."

They sat in intimate silence until the monitor chimed once again. Wander sighed and fitted the headset back on. "Be there with me," he asked.

"For as long as I am able," she whispered, her gaze only for him.

At the ten-minute count, Guns passed on shield control to the onboard computers and to the captain, while keeping a third key directly under his left hand. The triple backup was established in case the vessel came under attack before one or more of them could react. Waiting until the pirates committed themselves before shielding to full strength, in order to halt any risk of their detecting the battle shield and safely fleeing, was the riskiest part of the whole plan.

That done, Guns ordered, "All right. Let's loose the ferrets."

His heart hammering, Rick followed the number three's lead and keyed in the circuit that connected him to the wider-ranging signals' tracking units. The ship's outer tracker spread indiscriminately in all directions. It was the weapons tracker's function to wait and listen while the signals officer filtered through all incoming sensory data, until the foe was identified. At that split second, the tracker homed in, locked on, and attacked.

"Five minutes," Signals announced, his voice crackling with tension.

"Status unchanged," Consuela repeated, her calm utterly at odds with the flight deck atmosphere. When Guns snorted his derision, Rick had to agree. How could she remain so unaffected by the coming battle?

"Better make sure nobody's dropped off," Captain Arnol announced. "Helmsman, give them another blast."

"Red alert. Red alert. Battle stations. Attack in three minutes and counting."

Rick allowed himself to sink down in his seat, as though melding with the yielding surface and drawing directly into the power circuitry. As the signals officer searched, he sensed as well as saw on the monitors the outer reaches of the equipment's capacity, finding only empty space.

"Two minutes."

Rick's console squealed an alert, and his weapons circuits blinked ready to be locked, as Signals shouted, "We have a lock. A definite lock."

"Identify!"

"Shielded vessel, silenced and not under power, one

minute ten seconds off the lightway."

"Weapons!" Guns shouted. "We confirm an armed vessel, Skipper! Their phasers are armed!"

"On my command!"

"In range in fifteen seconds and counting!"

"Shields on fu—"

Then they were struck, and struck hard.

—Nineteen—

Perhaps it was because Rick did not know enough to keep careful hold of his weapons station. Perhaps it was his youth. Perhaps it was because of who he was and where he came from. Whatever the reason, Rick managed to fend off the stunners for the single instant required.

Barely.

A blinding flash of crackling energy exploded through the flight deck. Flickering blue tentacles of lightning raced up the consoles and passed through every body. The weapons lieutenant was blasted clear of his straps and halfway over his console. The number three screamed in agony and covered his eyes. Guns bellowed and went slack. Rick was aware of an awful pain searing his brain and locking his muscles down tight, yet still he somehow managed to hold his focus.

The moment before being struck, he had been glorying in the thrill of a surprise attack. His tracking system was focused down tightly on the ship, and as he monitored his tracking controls he was also extended outward, the warrior creeping up toward the enemy, weapons at the ready. In the span of two heartbeats he saw how the lieutenant honed in on the band of power that belted the ship's lower base, locking his weaponry on target, waiting for Guns to fire his neutron cannon and blow the shield. He saw how the number three had his weapons trained on the vessel's silent trail, where only a thin stream of emitted energy gave notice that the vessel was powered up to full, ready to move in for the kill.

But just as Guns prepared to blow the shield, Rick saw a bluish ball of energy race across the distance separating them and strike the nose of their own ship. In his convulsion, Guns fired off one cannon, and as the pain mounted in Rick's skull he saw the missile strike the shield a glancing blow, exactly as Guns had intended. The pirate's shield exploded in a fiery cloud of sparks, and the kinetic energy sent the vessel spinning slightly, so that the pirate's second stunner shot up and over their ship's nose.

Rick did not give it any conscious thought whatsoever. Screaming his rage and his determination not to give in to the pain, he locked in his controls to the lieutenant's tracking and weapons, and fired.

Their vessel shuddered under the backlash from firing three massive phaser bolts at once. Rick shouted his defiance as the bolts blasted their target, melting a glowering red belt around half of the pirate ship's lower base.

Guns heaved a heavy groan and struggled up in his seat.

"The controls! Get the controls!" Rick screamed, scarcely hearing himself as he worked to pull over the number three's tracking and weapons. As the pirates fired their thrusters, Rick's second batch of missiles smashed in and melted the tubes closed.

"They're rotating!" Guns roared, his fingers stabbing at his own power deck.

"Got 'em!" Rick shouted, racing against the menace of non-damaged weapons being rotated into firing position.

As the undamaged side of the pirate ship came into view, Rick fired a third volley, in sync with the stun-bolt blasted off by Guns. They shouted their defiant glee as the molten belt extended fully around the pirate's weaponry, and glimmers of angry lightning raced up and down the ship's surface.

"Firing second stunners!" Guns shouted, and again the blue-white powerball blasted the pirate's nose, sending the lancing light-traces along and through the ship.

"Hold your fire," Arnol ordered hoarsely. "Helmsman."

"He's still out, Skipper."

"Take over, Lieutenant. Retrace to the near point and hold position. Guns, train all weapons on the vessel."

"Aye, aye, Captain."

"Skipper," the junior signals officer announced, "we are receiving a distress call."

"Order them to surrender. Keep alert, Guns, this may be a ruse." He stabbed his console. "Chief Petty Officer, are you there?"

"Partly, Skipper. Only partly. What happened?"

"We took a stun-bolt direct amidships, but it looks like we survived and conquered. How's our battle readiness?"

There was a longish pause, then, "Couldn't muster more than half the main force, Captain. Maybe not even that."

"Captain," the junior signals officer announced, "they accept our surrender demand."

"Hold to your weapons, Guns."

"Finger's on the trigger, Captain."

"What's their attack status?"

"No sign of power to any weapons system."

"Order them to power down, suit up, open all bay doors, and bring all uninjured personnel into the outer holds where they are visible." He keyed and demanded, "You hear that, Chief Petty Officer?"

"Aye, Skipper." Life and strength were returning to Tucker's voice.

"Ready your men's weapons and suits." Arnol looked down and ordered, "Signals, inform me the instant their power is fully damped. Helmsman, at that point, I want you to extend the gravity net and draw them close enough for us to fasten a line."

"Power damped, Skipper. Bay doors opening."

"Gravity net extending, Captain."

"Full shield, Guns. Defense perimeter on attack."

"We're ready, Skipper."

"All right. Tuck, prepare to board and take prisoners." He glanced around. "And have a medic sent to the flight deck. We've got seven, no eight, wounded up here."

"Ten," Rick corrected, his gut clenching at the sight of Wander and Consuela sprawled motionless half-on and half-off their dais, their limbs intertwined. Even unconscious, they remained together.

–Twenty–

The lean, dark man and the wizened, old crone both wore the black robes of diplomats, with shoulders and sleeves chased in the silver filigree of senior rank. They gave the scarcest of bows before the Prince Commander's desk and announced, "We have news."

"I assumed nothing less," the Starfleet commander replied dryly, "given the fact that you insisted on seeing me without delay, despite the fact that we are currently engaged in three major conflicts."

Ignoring his sarcasm, the man stated, "Our monitors report that someone seeks to trod the forbidden ways."

The Prince Commander leaned back in his seat. "This is not what I wish to hear. Especially now."

"They have not yet found the door," the crone reported. "Yet they seek."

The Prince Commander, distant heir to the Hegemony throne and Commander of His Majesty's Sixth Battle Fleet, rose from his seat and began pacing the cold stone floor. He positively loathed the Starfleet command station for this quadrant, for that matter, and was immensely glad that he did not have to appear more than once or twice each

Standard year. The only reason he came at all was because it housed the training quarters for Talents.

His fortress possessed the charm and ambiance of a deserted tomb. The walls were thick and overly high, constructed of close-fitting, reddish gray stone. Interior and exterior were totally unadorned. The hallways were long and windowless and winding and narrow, filled with the anguish of all Talents who had been trapped and tortured there in eons past. The Prince Commander did not object to the years of rigid disciplining forced upon all Talents. He merely objected to having it under his command.

To make matters worse, the senior diplomats who were assigned liaison duty between the Talent station and his own command positively made his skin crawl.

From the relative safety of his office's most distant corner, he demanded, "So these forbidden ways do truly exist? I always thought they were the stuff of legends."

"That a man of your rank and station might consider them mere legends," the crone replied, swiveling upon a cane whose handle was carved from a single jewel, "is a testimony to the thoroughness with which we serve the Hegemony."

"Of course," the Prince Commander acquiesced. "So we are faced with the threat of a renegade Talent."

"Perhaps," the crone corrected. "It appears so."

"Appears? You're not sure?"

"We have lost contact with one of our ally vessels. And now we are picking up strange news. Rumors of a freighter inbound for Avanti with a captured pirate vessel."

"Impossible."

The other diplomat was a shrewd and ambitious man who ruled the planetary station with an iron fist. He tolerated the foul conditions only because his future advancement was at stake. "My monitors claim that it is so."

"Then your monitors have made a mistake."

"Doubtful," the crone quavered. "Most doubtful. These Talents guard their right to utilize the system's most powerful mind-amps with great zealousness."

The Prince Commander inspected his appearance in the full-length mirror. The tailored white robe hung most attractively over his corpulent form. The belt of woven gold managed to draw in his distended belly, and the high jeweled collar hid his chin's multiple folds. "If that is the case—"

"Then it is only a matter of time before the door is breached and the forbidden ways trod once more," the crone droned ominously.

"I suppose I must alert Central Starfleet Command," the Commander muttered, shuddering at the thought of bearing such news to the Prince Regent. Then he had an idea. "But you say that these are mere rumors?"

"That is so."

"Then perhaps the renegade can be eliminated before confirmation has been received. That is, if he exists at all."

"Difficult in the extreme," the male diplomat protested.

"Yes, or captured by other pirates," the Prince Commander went on happily.

"We have done as ordered," the lean man retorted. "We have come to you with news of possible renegade Talents. What you do with this news is up to you."

The crone wheeled to face her associate and protested, "But this is a Talent we are discussing!"

"A *renegade* Talent," he countered.

"Yet a Talent just the same. No one else could have detected the forbidden way and done so without monitoring equipment!"

"If it was done at all," he responded.

"Whether or not the rumors are true must be checked

out thoroughly," the crone snapped back. "But if they are, such a Talent must be brought to us and utilized!"

"Your report is duly noted," the Prince Commander said cheerfully, delighted at the sight of diplomats quarreling among themselves. They and the sensitives were the scourge of the empire, the lot of them.

He returned to his desk and seated himself. "Naturally, I could not take such a report to Starfleet Command without further verification. But in the meantime, I want you to use all powers at your disposal to eradicate this threat, if it exists at all. Yes. Then I should be able to report that the threat was noted and corrected. Is that understood? Very well. Then, you are dismissed."

– Twenty-one –

Rick keyed the door and announced, "Ensign Richard reporting as ordered."

"Enter."

He walked in and stood stiffly at attention. "You wanted to see me, Captain?"

"That's right." Flanking the captain were the senior helmsman, his head swathed in bandages, the senior weapons officer, and the acting signals officer, and power control officer—their superiors were still laid up. "Have a seat, Ensign."

"Thank you, Captain."

The captain's quarters were both large and sumptuous, compared to the rest of the ship. A polished table extended the length of the carpeted front room, a console flanking the captain's head position. Two side alcoves contained softly glowing light-sculptures. Rows of framed commendations rose above the bookshelves. Ornate panels separated this room from the captain's private quarters.

"Guns has been relating to us your actions, or as much as he can remember. I want you to tell me what happened."

Rick swallowed. The stern visages facing him gave no

indication as to whether they meant to reward him or demand his summary resignation. "It's all a little fuzzy, Captain."

"Take your time. Try to make it as complete as you can."

Rick struggled to make sense of the flurry of images. So much, so incredibly much had been packed into a battle that had scarcely lasted twenty seconds. He finished lamely, "I've probably forgotten something important, but I think that's everything."

Captain Arnol nodded once and glanced back down at the papers before him. "Your records indicate that other than your inbound transport, this is your first voyage into space. And that up to now you have received no formal training, as it was not available on your homeworld."

"I guess that's all pretty much true, Captain," Rick replied feebly.

"This beats all I've ever heard," the helmsman muttered.

"I agree," the captain said. "Yet nonetheless we must accept the fact that we are all alive and here today because of this young man's swift actions. Ensign, I am entering into your permanent records that your handling of this emergency saved the life of every man and woman on this ship."

"Thank you, Captain," Rick managed.

"Furthermore, as soon as we dock I am sending a message to Starfleet Command recommending that you be put up for the Medal of Valor. The recommendation will bear the signature of every officer on this ship."

To that Rick could find no reply.

"On behalf of all who serve under me, I extend to you my heartiest thanks and congratulations." The captain rose to his feet, and all followed his lead. "I am hereby granting you a temporary battlefleet promotion to lieutenant, and assigning you full watch status as Fourth Weapons Officer. This ship normally does not hold such a position, but I want you to go on record as a watch officer, and Guns says he would be willing to add you to his group."

"Proud to stand with him," the veteran growled. "Very proud."

"I have searched the records and found nothing to suggest that an ensign has ever been granted a battlefleet promotion even before cadet training, and there is every likelihood that this decision will be overturned when you return to Fleet Command. But nonetheless it will remain on your record. And if I have anything to do with it, your actions will go down in battlefleet history as an example which other ensigns should strive to follow."

Arnol stood, picked up a small wooden box from his console, walked over, and handed it to Rick. "Your bars of rank, Lieutenant. Wear them with pride."

Rick looked down at the shining silver bars, and for a moment they seemed to shimmer before his eyes. He struggled to mouth the words, "Thank you, Captain."

"You have earned them." The captain marched back to his place, and still at attention, announced, "Dismissed, Lieutenant."

In a daze, Rick walked back out into the passage. He leaned against the wall and felt a sudden surging desire to run and share the news with someone, anyone who could share the thrill and make it real.

Almost without realizing it, he found himself walking down the corridor and entering sickbay. The medic gave him a friendly nod, noted the bars on his shoulders, and grinned. "The skipper did it, then. Congratulations."

"The whole crew knows about it?"

"Everybody who can walk and talk. You're the hero of the hour." He sobered as his glance shifted to the door behind him. "You and the pair in there."

"How are they?"

"Hard to tell. The girl's from your homeworld, I hear."

"That's right."

The medic walked over, keyed the door, motioned Rick forward. "Hard to know exactly what's up with a sensitive who's been power fried, so I've let them sleep and just kept a careful watch."

The sickbay was crammed with beds and patients. Rick craned through the doorway, saw the two motionless forms lying in beds set side by side, both surrounded by softly beeping monitors. "She looks so pale."

"Deep sleep," the medic said calmly. Clearly he was not worried. "Done a little checking. Best thing that can happen under the circumstances, or so the books say. They both woke up a couple of times and drank some water, with my help of course. Even said a couple of words to each other. Almost as though each came back just to make sure the other was doing all right." The medic smiled a second time. "Never thought I'd see the day when I would care about a pilot's health."

"Scouts," Rick corrected, and for some reason felt a pang of jealousy. Not at the attention given these two, but rather over the feelings they showed for each other, even here, even now.

"Not anymore," the medic replied. "Not in my book. Anybody who's done what they've done deserves the full ranking." He gave the pair of beds a confident nod. "Give them time, they'll come around. They're strong, they're sharp, and they've got the greatest reason of all to recover."

"What's that?"

The medic's third grin was the biggest of all. "Love."

Consuela drifted in and out of sleep, moving back and forth in a rushing surge of waves. Steady and deep, carrying her away and then returning. She heard the calm voices, did not care to focus and listen, because to do so would mean rising to full consciousness. And she was not ready for that. Not yet.

She felt the reassuring return of strength to her limbs, and the gradual easing of the pain in her mind. The shock had been staggeringly powerful, but the memory of her experience in the training hall helped her cope. That and Wander's presence. She had woken up several times, managed to turn her head and see that he was there and resting easily, even spoken to him once. For the moment, it was enough.

She heard a voice she recognized as Rick's, and took comfort from his presence as well. Then she was away, swept back into the sea of sleep. But this time there was a difference.

The flowing up and out and away was stronger this time, carrying her farther and farther from the bed and the sickbay and the voices. Farther still, a current so powerful she was helpless to resist, sweeping her back in calm and fluid power.

Toward home.